Child of These Tears

Child of These Tears

a novel

Molly McNett

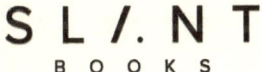

SL/NT
BOOKS

CHILD OF THESE TEARS
a novel

Slant Books
P.O. Box 60295
Seattle, WA 98160

www.slantbooks.org

Cataloguing-in-Publication data:

Names: McNett, Molly.

Title: Child of these tears: a novel / Molly McNett.

Description: Seattle, WA: Slant Books, 2025

Identifiers: ISBN 978-1-63982-203-4 (hardcover) | ISBN 978-1-63982-202-7 (paperback) | ISBN 978-1-63982-204-1 (ebook)

Subjects: LCSH: United States--History--Colonial period, ca. 1600-1775--Fiction | Iroquois Indians--Fiction | Jesuits--In literature | Captivity narratives

For Katie

Although I have walked in these woods,
how can I claim to love them?
One by one I shall forget the names of individual things.
You who sleep in my breast are not met with words.

—Guigo the Angelic,
Ninth Prior of the Grande Chartreuse monastery

13 October 1703

To His Excellency Joseph Dudley
His Majestie's Governor for the Province
of Massachusetts Bay
in the English America

Sir,

You have, of course, been made aware of the fearsome state of affairs in Hartfield Falls since the start of *Queen Anne's War*. Three of our flock were carried off last month by a small party of *Indians* on behalf of the *French*, and all of our means spent in repairs and fortifications. Therefore, I request that our poor Hamlet be exempt from the Country Rates, and provided with muskiteers in the number of twenty, and ten dogs withal to keep the guard, and to give chase to the enemy, if what we dread in fear and trembling should come to pass.

I am, Sir, with infinite respect
Yr Very Hbe Sert,
John Baker
Hartfield Falls

Constance Baker, eight years of age

SHE CLEAVED HERSELF in two. The wicked part she hid from Mother and Father, but when it grew angry, or showed its greed or immoderate affection, she was ashamed, and wished that the wicked part would perish, along with all sinful things.

But perhaps she did not truly wish this. She loved many sinful things.

She loved nonsensing. This was spinning to make herself dizzy, while saying the words of her catechism, *out of his mere good pleasure pleasure pleasure,* until the word was like the buzzing of bees and she laughed and toppled over.

She loved bacon fat. She put the fat in the soap, as Mother told her to do, and only then licked her fingers and found it very good and delightful.

She loved her brother John, but she hated him, too, for he pushed her when Mother could not see, and was not punished, and though he was very much younger than she, one whole year younger, he was permitted to carve a toy musket with Father's good knife, with its shining blade that ended in a shelf, a seat for a tiny fairy, while she was only permitted the wooden scutching knife.

She loved the baby Ezariah, for his square head sat directly on his shoulders, his soft neck hidden like a turtle's, and he was suffered to gurgle and burp and spit, and make all manner of loud noises. And she did not mind if he pulled her hair or squirmed when she held him tight with much cherishing. Each day when she woke, she remembered him, and was happy in him, which in itself was not wicked, only that during her chores she must run to kiss him.

But children could not be very happy for long, it seemed, for they must cleave themselves in two and the wicked parts would leave their chores to kiss the baby, or ask to keep a housecat, then ask again when they had been refused, which exercised their parents and proved the children to be enemies of God, given to disobeying and nonsensing and licking bacon fat.

Then Mother furrowed her brow and looked wearily at her (she wiped her shining lips on her sleeve but it was too late) and handed her the good knife, saying "Cut a switch." Then the wicked girl cut a very green and soft switch so that her mother must instead beat her with an open palm, which stung terribly. But the girl knew, at least, to be quiet, for there would come more blows if she did not.

From the Relation of What Occurred in the Mission of St. Ignace at La Rivière des Anges in the Year 1702; Letter of Father Simon René Floquart to the Reverend Father Superior of the Missions of the Society of Jesus in New France

Reverend Father in Christ
The Peace of Christ!
Praise the Lord for all is well if He is by!

IT HAS BEEN raining and so difficult to visit our savages, as the little paths are very muddy. For this reason I have requested another pair of shoes, identical to the ones sent last year, so I can allow one to dry while wearing the other; it is difficult to clean them while the mud is fresh. Also, as it has been related, the mosquitos at this time of year are the size of hummingbirds. The last time I took the path, my face was swollen so badly from bites the savages laughed at me, saying I had "forgotten to bring my eyes," as I understood them. Later that day I sprinkled the path with holy water, but these insects still form dark clouds above it, they are so plentiful. As the Son of God is given us through suffering, my soul receives Him here in abundance. (Father Baudoin, in his recent visit, mentioned a tree on the island of *New Holland* whose oil is said to repel mosquitos quite magically. I suppose it is costly but if some can be secured for our mission we might save those souls who still await a "true miracle" to consent to baptism.)

Once I reach their longhouses the mosquitos lessen due to the fire inside; as my predecessors have mentioned, even the savages have difficulty breathing in these structures; the smoke is thick, the stench of bear grease, which they use upon their hair, is rancid and overpowering; the eyes water, and one cannot stand erect because the only air that is fit to breathe is just at ground level. If it is raining, I find them all inside, lying prone and pressing their mouths to the earth. But they never complain—at least, as far as I can understand them.

My attempts at their language open me to further ridicule, but I won't elaborate here except to report that they now call me *Simon le Gros*, or *Père le Gros*, as the little French they have learned, they use to insult and tease. I bear it as a sort of *agere contra*; and also because I must gain their affection and confidence in any way I can, and it is fit to mention only because at the recent feast held for the Assumption, they took my best cassock and fitting two of them inside it—it is commodious even for such a robe, however—they began a merry *dance*, hopping on the right foot and leaning that way, then the left, I suppose to imitate my "waddling"; followed by rude gestures I cannot mention here, but which reduced them all to tears of laughter. The garment was torn in several places, and of the 33 buttons only 12 remain. I have one spare soutane, but as with my shoes, I must wear one while drying the other, which takes a long time in the humid climate, and the mud is impossible to avoid.

For these reasons I request a new soutane of identical size and quality—the measurements follow. For the buttons, it is best if they are firmly sewn, and sent with needles and thread to sew them on again when they come loose.

It is true that the Roman garment is not standard to our order, yet I hope it is no vanity on my part to wear it, as you may have suggested. The belt of the standard soutane I wore previously was stolen by the savages for an eye-bandage, and any replacement would suffer a similar fate; also, the buttons of the Roman style are most useful to demonstrate the years of Christ's life. (Yet I found two of my buttons in the headdress of a savage who insisted he had traded at Montréal for them!)

In addition, please send a hat to replace the one I currently wear, as well as another to use when I am not wearing it, for they disdain baldness or thinning hair and it is dangerous for them to see my naked head. On one occasion when I was sleeping they drew in ink the likeness of a plump goose upon my head, and other *bêtises* followed, such as their children stealing my needles as I took my afternoon repose, and all in concert "poking the goose"; that is, pricking the skin of my head, and with the blood they had drawn, painting his "feathers." The skin near the neck of the goose—on the crown of my head—may be scarred permanently. Our savages never reprimand their children, and when I explained to them what the young ones had done, all laughed very evilly and not one of them defended me.

Of course, all the things I have requested will be worth nothing without your prayers for the souls of the heathen we baptize here.

Yours in Our Lord,
Simon René Floquart, missionary

John Baker, His Commonplace Book
with Lucubrations
by many great men of learning

Vox audita perit, littera scripta manet;
The word that is heard perishes,
but the letter that is written abides.

6 July, 1701

JUST ONE YEAR ago in this hamlet of Hartfield Falls in the English America, our dear Reverend *Woodbridge* did perish in the night when his house burned to the ground. Yet miraculously one room remained unscathed, which contained some one hundred various books. This little library was in itself a miracle, the only one of its kind in the new world.

Surely Providence has spared these volumes so that we who remain might preserve what is contained within them. For it is said that when the Great Library of Alexandria burned, it set back the knowledge of man by one thousand years.

I proceed here as Seneca, in the manner of a bee buzzing from flower to flower to collect their nectar, including verses most helpful for consolation, wonders and mysteries of science, advices, voyages and peoples various, as well as fishes and animals of the good earth that be mostly known.

I shall commit these selections to memory withal, so that they may be preserved if the dark day comes, and my own house burns in the night (yet, being stone, it is difficult to fire) or if we are set upon by the enemy, and I am unable to tuck this book under an arm in my elopement.

May the Lord spare us that dark day. May He blot our enemies from the book of the living, so that we may serve Him forever in peace.

ARTS (domestic)

Making soap in the new of the moon may make no difference in its coming, but it certainly does no harm.

CHILDREN

(Below some advice on their rearing, which may be read by parents, or aloud to small children themselves.)

Per INCREASE MATHER, Preacher of the Gospel of Christ
Go into secret corners and plead it with God . . . if you dy and be not first new Creatures, better you had never been born. Your godly Parents will testifie against you before the Son of God at that day and if you dy in a Christless, graceless estate, I will most certainly profess unto Jesus Christ at the day of *Judgement*, Lord, these are the Children, whome I spake often unto thy Name, publickly and privately, and I told them that if they did not make themselves a new heart they should become damned creatures for evermore; and yet they would not repent and believe the Gospel.

Per JOHN ROBINSON, preacher
And surely there is in all children a stubbornness, and stoutness of mind arising from natural pride, which must be broken and beaten down. For the beating and keeping down of this stubbornness parents must provide two things: first that children's wills and *willfullness* be restrained and repressed. . . . The second help is an inuring of them from the first, to such a meanness in all things, as may rather pluck them down, than lift them up.

~

8

CHILDREN ctd

Below, if the reader will permit me, I add an account of my daughter Constance, aged 1 yr. 3 mo.

After she had been walking several months, and she understood yes and no and what I would have her do, she refused a crust of her morning bread that her mother had given her, perhaps because it was hard, or that it had an unfamiliar shape, and so she threw it to the floor and would not take it back. Then I took her to the cellar, for she was afraid of that dark place, and told her gently that she would take the crust from me, and obey me. Again she grabbed this crust and threw it down, and sobbed immoderately and cried out with a devilish voice. So I locked her in that dark place, though fearing that as she could now toddle across a room, she might climb the stairs and fall, I blocked the stairs with a board. Then I returned every hour or two in that long day to speak most gently with her and tell her that she had disobeyed me (and she could speak, and understood yes and no and knew my meaning) and that if she would take the bread and eat it, and embrace me, she might come upstairs again. Again and again she refused it. By the end of the day she was limp and worn from crying, and finally did take the water I offered and eagerly snatched the crust and ate it, but when I held out my arms to her, she turned her head away most wickedly and would not embrace me, and so I left her there in that cellar until the morning, and God saw fit to enter her that night, so that the next morning I found her curled on the floor and she raised her arms to me, and I gathered her to me, and thanked the Lord that after this day she did in all things obey me, or if she did not, one beating would suffice to remind her, so that her tears had been her blessing.

Pleiades (misc./sciences)

Per NEWMAN'S *News from the Stars*
Time out of mind there has seven Stars bin observed in the Pleiades, and at Present there is to be seen but six, a very probable sign that one of them is retired and become invisible.

From the *Journal Intime*
of Father Simon René Floquart

TODAY I WENT out in the rain carrying the new wax-coated parasol, feeling as I walked that I was struggling with a live thing, due to the force of the wind which lifted it powerfully until I must use both hands to draw it down and found myself engaged in such a struggle I no longer advanced on the trail, and imagined Father Dublon watching me and laughing at my "contest" with this implement. ("Is it not for the ladies?" he teased me, although I had found its bright cherry color quite pleasing and cheerful.) Again it seemed everything conspired against me—the rain, the wind, the very tool which was to prove useful against them, and I felt my teeth grinding. It is not the first time that I attempt here to do something to make myself more at ease, then the failure of that attempt causes me more aggravation than simply enduring the original offense. (My self-styled "swatter" against the black flies, etc.) The Lord in His insistence that I must surrender to the life here? Again I wonder why it is that I am troubled by these minor irritations, which I know very well have no importance in God's eyes. And my reverie of martyrdom, my fascination with the glorious men who come before me, seem childish to me; I remind myself that it is necessary to brave much discomfort before one could *possibly be worthy in God's eyes to spill one's blood for Him*, that in fact I seem to be stuck in the second mansion (as it is described by St. Teresa of Ávila); and even wondering about my place in such and such a mansion is evidence of my distracted thinking. (The *beginner* doubts and feels discouraged and compares himself with others. Then he goes beyond that, to the experience, which can and does comprise *everything*. Devoutly to be wished!) Even my dejection at this thought is not His intention, however.

Father Dublon is so kind that one could never fault him; if he laughs at me it is in a spirit of brotherhood, for his eyes shine with the clarity of the most devout. There is no hardness or impatience in them. This peace comes to those who have given up the expectations of this world and rest in the next.

Yet neither of us could compare to our early Fathers of New France. How these devout men endured privations, how they of necessity forged the way through the wilderness, how they made the first forays into the savage tongue, and, most of all, faced death and torture at the hands of infidels, how truly they were *made a spectacle to the world, to angels and to men*. What role do we play, then, Father Dublon and I? We have discomforts, even squalor by the standards of the old country. But the glory is not ours; we are only tasked with maintaining what they have achieved.

For many years I have imagined my mother's response to my discontent, so that while the sound of her worldly voice has escaped my memory, there is another, timeless one I have fostered within: "My son! You are saving the souls of these dear savages." I must not forget that this is the goal of our mission here, and not the *spectacle of men*. Yes, to perish in the name of our Lord and in the exercise of charity—this is all I wish. However, it seems I am unlikely even to die as Father Noüe, to be sent into the wilderness, to lose my way, and to be found frozen to death while kneeling in prayer. Even this seems beyond reach.

Last night I dreamt that some other savage tribe—the Hurons, perhaps—came to make war on our outpost. Everywhere our poor savages had fallen bleeding on the paths. I hid myself in some bushes, in the manner of Father Jogues, but instead of rushing forward to aid the savages in Christian death as he had done, I remained hidden, from cowardice. Yet the hem of my soutane was oddly long, like a tail, so that, seeing where it trained over the path, the Hurons pulled it, dragged me forward, tied me to a stake, and there cut off my lips and tongue, just as we know from the Relations (and from the eyewitness of several savages worthy of belief) they *truly did* to Father Brébeuf.

What I recall most vividly from this part of the dream was not the pain of the knife, nor the blood which ran over my eyes in a cataract, but that in my great suffering I was struck dumb. I knew that I should call to God, to groan and cry out to Him continually, as Father Brébeuf had done. And yet no sound came.

It was this muteness that brought about such dread that I woke from the dream, sitting up with a start. Then what disappointment came over me! The blood I had felt running down my face was only my own perspiration under the mosquito netting.

How are we to understand Christ's suffering if not through the body? Otherwise it is only conjecture. When I wake on my soft bed, I feel a disgust for my own corpse and its love of comfort; and the mosquito netting seems the very veil that prevents me from seeing Him clearly.

O God, send what you will to draw me closer to you!

Help me to be worthy of glorious suffering!

Constance

SHE WAS VERY happy, for a dog had come to the house. She sat with him in the long grass where the deer lay at night and pressed it down, and turned her head so that he might lick her face and breathe into her ear with a shudder, which was most delightful. And she wanted to remember forever and ever sitting on the grass with the dog on the day that they had named him General. And his shuddering breath, and the warm sun, and when she closed her eyes, the blue and pink beams on her eyelids.

But there were many days and many moments and minutes within each day, and already very many of these she had forgotten, as if they had never happened.

This was a troubling thing.

If her mind were a house, every thing might have its place within. In the upper chamber, perhaps, the people she knew. In the parlor, all sums and numbers to one-thousand. The corner pantry for doing-things. How to darn, take a stitch-in-place, to dye and starch, each on a shelf beside the pewter plates and cups, and the stone jugs with their handles like little ears.

In the attic, beside the wooden beehives, were *those things that had passed.* But as there were so very many things that had passed, her mind sent some, without her knowing, to the cellar.

This was a dark place where she could not go. But moments and minutes went there, and people withal. For example, her sister Hannah, one of the Holy and Exemplary Christian Children, whom she did not remember.

The Commonplace Book of John Baker

CHILDREN (ctd.)

I beg the reader to permit me one more account, that shows us
how children may please the Lord in their death (and something
very like, I observed at the death of a daughter, *Hannah*).

Per JAMES JANEWAY, Minister Of The Gospel (from *A Token
for Children, being an Exact Account of the Conversion, Holy and Exemplary Lives and Joyful Deaths of Several YOUNG CHILDREN*)

Mary, 5 years of age

On the Lord's day she was left alone at home and instead of playing (as other naughty children use to do) she told them "That
was the Lord's Day and that they ought to remember that day to
keep it Holy": and then she told them how it was to be kept in re-
ligious exercise all the day long except so much as was to be taken
up in the works of Necessity and Mercy ... she took great part in
the reading of Scripture and some Part of it was more dear to her
than her appointed Food. . . . She was not many days sick before
she was marked, and was greatly rejoiced to think that she ... was
now going to Christ. . . . Being desired by the standers by, to give
them a particular Account of what she saw: she answer'd, *You shall
know hereafter*; and so in an extasy of Joy and holy Triumph, she
went to Heaven. . . .

HALLELUJAH

15

God's great Providence and enduring mercies as occasioned
by the terable captivitie and wonderfull redemption of
Sarah Baker (John Baker his wife) of Hartfield Falls,
the Colony of Massachusetts Bay in the English America,
having been captivated by most barbarous salvages and
carried, with her daughter, to Canada

ON THE 27th day of the month called February, 1703/4, I, Sarah Baker, was awakened, together with my family, by the sound of gunfire outside the palisade of our village. It was early morning and dim. We were ten people in that house, viz., myself, my husband, my sister and her boys, my children, and three soldiers stationed there for our protection. Hard upon the first noises my husband therefore, dressing, taking up his pistol, and uttering a prayer for our safety withal, ran from the garrison to join the counterforce, who gathered in order to stave off the barbarians before they breached our fortifications.

The children were also awakened at the loud reports of these guns, and a hallowing and screeching which grew ever closer. We were in our bed clothes, all. Which was more difficult to calm at that time, the children or my poor sister, a widow, who exclaimed and cried that my husband had left us defenseless there in that house, I cannot say. Though the soldiers were armed and ready; yet soon the hallowing and shrieks did grow closer until we sensed the enemy was hard upon our garrison house; we hid ourselves under the beds in the upper chamber and the children at first kept quiet admirably, the infant by its sucking; yet my dear son John, being held by his sister, did break free of her grasp, and eloped, running down the stairs to

16

come to the aid of his father; great fear came over us as the front door was tomahawked, and one soldier fallen at the threshold, one shot through the bowels, the other taking one ball in his breast and one in the face, whereat my sister's children could not be prevailed upon to stay quiet in our hiding place and began screeching. O, terrible day! How our breasts burst in fear as, on a sudden, our house was beset by these hideous salvages, perhaps six or seven, though I was not sensible enough to count at that time, being quite overcome. I stood before the bed under which my daughter Constance hid, as the killdeer draws the fox away from its nest (my infant perforce, tucked under one wing) yet, on a sudden I fell in a swoon. Moments later I perceived that they dragged me by the hair, and bound me; when I came to senses I saw the infant lay motionless, its face very much mutilated; it being eight months of age, born in the month called *July*. Only with God's grace was I able to quell my cries, and reason that its squealing had angered them and caused its death; therefore, I held my tongue, standing dumbly as my daughter Constance was likewise dragged from under the bed, but as one devil came forward to pinion her, I had the presence of mind to command her to "keep quiet" which order she did obey, being 8 years of age and tractable, at that time, in all things; and God did stave their hands to spare her life.

Not so my poor sister, who, crying out for her sons, whom these brutes had tomahawked, was similarly dispatched, though I did not witness the foul deed as I was bound and my face to the floor. Only later I learned too that my son John, who had bravely sought to exit the palisade to come to his father's aid, as I have told, and crawling under, where it rotted, as he squirmed there, one of the devils dealt a blow to his pate; now I hope, he is gathered back to the Lord; he was seven years of age and, just one month before the terable day, still wore a dress.

One faithful dog General took a ball in the side; we passed it lying by the way.

O, reader! What sorrow descended upon my heart; notwithstanding the Lord showed tremendous mercy for I did not all together lose my head; fain did I commit my fate unto Him, and that of my daughter and of my son and of my husband, who had gone I knew not whither.

Now my bonds were loosed in order for me to dress, and to dress my Constance for she was rendered insensible by the carnage at our feet. Verily, I should not have been sensible but that I had a duty to my child; I knew as I dressed her, both of us trembling before the faces that looked on, their shining blades in hand, that divine providence had preserved her.

What a sight, when we were led from the house, to see the village fired hither and yon, shrouded in smoke; lambs, hogs, cattle running wild, grazing and scratching as they pleased as though they ran the town, and their former masters pinioned, or lying dead on the ground, those dear souls to whom just yesterday we had spoken of things light and worldly!

We were led downstairs and out, to the center of the village, and by the way we came upon the body of my poor son John, and those of his cousins, at which I gave thanks to God that my poor sister was spared the sight.

Reader, what a doleful, amazing, woeful sight His chosen people made then, corralled, shivering, in the middle of our haven. I found myself alongside Mistress Kimball. She had given my babe its first nursing, her travail coming just five weeks before mine. We were pinioned both, our arms behind, and came to stand together. We did not speak, for our arms were empty, therefore we knew what had passed, and were for one another, as those who sat with Job seven days and seven nights and *no one spoke a word, for they knew his pain was very great.*

Then other neighbors came to the circle; all bound, yet our captors suffered us to speak; we enjoined one another to submit to the Lord, and put our trust in Him. I said, perchance my husband John is also with the Lord; yet they told me he may yet live for some had seen him. (I learned later, this God graciously vouchsafed.)

The Commonplace Book of John Baker

HELP ME O Lord, for I am downcast. Thus I prayed and He lifted my trembling hand to the book I must read, and turned its pages, and trained my dull red eye upon the part that He would have me relay here—

Per JOHN FLAVEL, preacher of the Gospel of Christ in *A Token for Mourners: or the advice of Christ to a distressed mother bewailing her dear and only son.*

It is common with men, yea, with good men, to exceed in their Sorrows for dead Relations, as it is to exceed in their Loves and delights to living Relations; and both of the one and other, we may say as we say of Waters, It's hard to contain them within their bounds. It is therefore grave advice which the Apostle delivers in this case, 1 Cor. 7:29-30: But this I say, Brethren, the time is short; It remaineth, that both they that have wives, be as though they had none; and they that weep, as though they wept not; and those that rejoyce, as though they rejoyced not.

From the *Journal Intime*
of Father Simon René Floquart

TODAY THE BEREAVED woman came to me, speaking excitedly. I was seated on the bench in the chapel, and she took my hand, pulled me to my feet, and uttered something that I did not understand, although after she repeated it many times, I realized she was not speaking the savage tongue, but *talitha cumi*, as she remembers anything I have told her, even if I do not recall having said it. She seemed to be asking me to do what Christ had done for the daughter of Jairus; that is, to go to the longhouse and say to her dead daughter, *Damsel, I say unto thee, arise.* I tried to explain to the woman that I did not have the power of Christ, and was only His servant, but she repeated again *talitha cumi*, and tugged forcefully on my hand.

I longed to rush in, to speak with her easily, as Father Dublon could have done, but found myself instead saying, You must only pray, or, rather, that one savage word which seems to incorporate all the other notions into the verb for praying.

But at this, her face lightened, and she left, mumbling the Pater Noster, and leaving me with a true sense of wonder. Without our initial struggle I might not have remarked on her understanding, and it seems that my own *ineptitude* causes me to be flooded with delight when I say something and it is understood—even the smallest thing!

It was God's design to confound our tongues at Babel so that we understood that it was not according to our own devices that we should proceed on this earth, but rather by trusting all to Him. And yet He provided, too, this mysterious way in which we are able, even haltingly, to build this tender bridge! If He withholds it from me, perhaps it is only to make me grateful when He gives it. And indeed, sometimes even when I say, *the peace of the Lord*, and they repeat it, I am most tenderly moved, even to tears.

Without our mission here, what hope had this woman and her poor daughter of ever seeing one another in heaven? To see His handiwork, and, for my part, to be well-used by Him in this way, is a delight which surpasses any other.

From . . . *the terable captivitie and wonderfull redemption of Sarah Baker*

First Remove

THEN WITH MY dear Constance at my skirts these savages led us out of our poor bewildered hamlet, smoking and smoldering now with the sun up about an hour. Our captors motioned us to the north and so we began, huddled together and marching in a line through the snow, then in perhaps an hour turning east to descend into the gorge at Thankfull Wood, a terrain still familiar, and up again, some times crawling to manage the snow, which was nearly to our knees, and through it all enjoined to hurry ever faster by our captors. There seemed to be an hundred souls there who marched in this long line; I later learned, a distance of thirteen miles, which then, because I was not inured to travel, and suffered the cold and snow and sore grief withal, seemed much more. But there would come greater trials indeed.

Mistress Kimball came in the same band, and though we marched single file yet I could see her ahead of me, and the snow stained some times with blood where she had passed. Constance was also before me, and I thanked God, for it was a comfort to me as though my eyes could offer her protection. As I was cold I knew she was too, our shoes and clothes ill suited to the snow and chill wind, but God gave her strength to bear it. Our captors prodded us along by gesture. One Frenchman spoke enough English to enjoin us to march "faster" which, the snow being several feet deep, and melting with the sun two or three hours high by then was very hard; which difficulty did not come close to what lay in store.

That day we came finally to an halt having passed through the Thankfull Gorge, to the far edge of that forest. We had come a long way, yet not so far, I hoped, that our men could not pursue the band and rescue us (though it was not to be.) We were sorely tired yet how should we sleep after what had passed, and being on the cold ground with only boughs between us and the snow, and nothing to keep us from the night wind? I was still pinioned, and Constance too lest she loose my bonds and help us to elope together as we had not yet entered the wilderness; there we lay shivering, for we were, as I have wrote, yet in our home garments, our stockings and shoes soaked from snow, no caps or cloaks and thinly clad; they made no fire so that we would not be spotted on our march; Constance still wore her night cap on her head, for which I was glad, being very cold about my own ears, my cap having fallen off by the way. Neither had we refreshment, for though they offered some jerked meat from their plunder, I had but little appetite, and Constance, much exercised with the day's amazement, could not be prevailed upon to eat.

There we lay upon those coarse boughs placed on the snow, where they had dug it out, and in our thin garments, and the cold coming on and pinioned so we could not warm one another, and all the day's sore trials came to the fore; Constance calling now and then "*Mother!*" as if to make certain that I, at least, remained alive, at her side, or perhaps wondering at her dear siblings now departed, which thought it pinched me to entertain. I thought, and did not say, with Job: *What I dread befalls me.*

Constance

SHE CLEAVED HERSELF in two, and tried to be the warm one God had made inside her. Heart and liver, bowels and blood. The warm part talked silently to the cold one, saying, go on, you must.

The body went, but the feet were unwell. They were of the cold part, yet they burned strangely, then crystals of ice entered them, and grew, pushing out her flesh and taking the room of it. So she stood on a chair, and took the numbers down from the parlor shelf, seven hundred twenty-four, seven hundred twenty-five, and up to one thousand, a very great number, and then down again, willing the feet to step with each number. When they stopped her mother put her feet near the fire. They burned, as if they were in the fire itself and not beside it, so that she cried out, and her mother pressed a hand over mouth and whispered fiercely that she must bear it, or incur the wrath of the master.

Again she cleaved herself in two. The quiet part was still as a hare. When her shoes came off, her feet were yellow.

From the *Journal Intime*
of Father Simon René Floquart

I AM LATELY disturbed by the immoderate grief of the savage woman. It should not surprise me, perhaps, for she has tended to extremes in worship, several times fasting to weakness, and whipping herself after Father Dublon told her that the Ursulines mortified the flesh in this manner. He is presently in Montréal for spiritual direction so I must decide how to proceed in this delicate matter, which is perhaps a greater grief because the dead daughter carried the family line of that longhouse. Now the bereaved woman has cut herself and refuses to dress the wounds, or even to eat, so that she is too weak to answer my questions—Are the wounds a means of supplication? What end has she in mind?— although I am not sure that I could understand her answer.

Women are, at times, given to extremes of devotion; they are able to affect the postures easily, but their minds are given to cloudiness and exaggeration.

My own mother is an exception, of course, yet once before going to sleep upon the floor by her bed, she rubbed nettles upon her skin. It disturbed me greatly when I saw the red and angry bumps on her arm, as I had helped her to gather these nettles by the stream! It was a sunny day, and we wore gloves, and talked comfortably. I had thought we were collecting the nettles for soup, and had taken pleasure in the task!

Of course, my mother had her wonderful end in mind, and I was merely ignorant of this at the time. Yet in the main I do not trust women, nor their self-imposed wounds, and I am not certain that such things are pleasing to the Lord.

I hope I do not say this out of jealousy of the savage woman, but I must consider that it is possible. Would I be able to cut my own scalp and refrain from stitching or dressing it as she has done? Now they tell me she is gravely ill and have promised to send for me if she worsens.

In the meantime I have been chopping wood for the chapel. I grew out of breath quickly today, while the savages who worked beside me never tired. Indeed they became more mischievous as our work wore on, stealing my axe when I rested, calling me *sag-amité*, corn pudding, poking my stomach and laughing. I detest being touched in the stomach, and pouted as I went, now fighting tears of anger, now brooding again on our great martyrs of New France, and my own inadequacy in the face of their example.

Father Brébeuf, using his own name for an epithet, called himself an ox who was fit only to haul heavy burdens, and his strength was sufficient to his task. But his Relations tell us that he truly longed for the grace of martyrdom, which he was ready to accept with joy and contentment. So that when the barbarians had cut away his lower lip and stuffed a hot iron down his throat, his only concern was with his superior, Father Lalemant, who suffered alongside him and was weaker in constitution! In the shadow of such men, we must conceive of more humble wishes; for mine, perhaps that I might receive the grace of patience to withstand discomfort. Yes, when I wrote in the Relation that I found *suffering* here in abundance, I should have written only this word, *discomfort*. In fact, the comforts I find here are just enough that I confound discomfort with true suffering.

Pray about this.

The Commonplace Book of John Baker

HOW MAY WE know, dear Reader, that the Lord chastens us?
Only now that the dark day has come, my Lord, does my eye see
Thee.

CHASTENING

Judges 2

2 And ye shall make no league with the inhabitants of this land;
ye shall throw down their altars: but ye have not obeyed my voice:
why have ye done this? 3 Wherefore I also said, I will not drive
them out from before you; but they shall be as thorns in your
sides, and their gods shall be a snare unto you.

From the *Confessions*
of Father Simon René Floquart, Part One

O LORD, you called my father to you when I was but eight years of age, and I do not remember him well. After his death, one early morning after having had a bad dream, and going to my mother as was my habit, I found her sleeping on the floor beside her bed.

During that night, my mother had been sent a vision of Sister Marie de L'Incarnation, whom you had called to establish the Ursuline convent in New France, some twenty years before that time. In this vision, Sister Marie stood shrouded in fog, as the mountaintops of New France rose up in the distance, and my mother heard her voice enjoining, *Do as I have done! Prepare your son for your departure.*

As you know, Lord, I did not learn any of this until much later, but only knew that my mother had changed toward me, for I was an only child (as my mother had been rendered barren in childbirth with me) and very much coddled; yet from that time she thought it best that I should not be touched in any way, which might have been difficult for some women, but you, O Lord, helped her to grow distant in her heart. I recall that it was forbidden to disturb her in contemplation, which time grew longer and longer, and I was overtaken by a foreboding most terrible and began to chew on my shirt sleeves. Yet, Lord, you saw to it that she did not remark on this, or reprimand me; it was my Aunt who later punished me for this *vilain défaut* when my mother gave me over to her care "for a time," as she entered the convent in Tours, and later made her preparations to go to the Ursulines in New France.

So it was, my God, that you wonderfully made use of my dear mother, and made her able to speak and write in the languages of the Huron and the Iroquois, and called upon her to save the souls of hundreds of savages in New France, and deliver them unto you. In this way she became a mother to many before she died!

I asked after my mother as the months went by and I had not received even a letter from her, but my aunt could not properly explain her whereabouts or her reasons to me, having twelve other children to care for. I did have the company of my cousins, which was a balm to me, and they accepted me as a brother and sometimes during our games and sport I forgot that heaviness in my breast which made life dolorous. But my aunt, perhaps instinctively, always fed me my portion last, and when the gruel ran out, poured hot water into the pan and scraped the bottom and stirred it for my portion, saying, this is the best I can do, with a sigh of real sorrow, but if it was for the fact that she had taken me on as a burden or that food was indeed scarce, I did not know. (Since the death of my father, my uncle had been burdened with two households, which forced my aunt to dismiss her *bonne*, and undertake all of the domestic chores herself, until his fortunes improved several years later. As she was unused to such work, my aunt must have been very tired, and when one is tired one is apt to become cross.)

When I remember this time, I feel a pinch in my stomach, as if I were still hungry enough to cry from the ache of it. I did often want to cry from hunger, and in those early days once burst into tears when I saw my bowl, at which my aunt told me that I must be stronger. She did not say it unkindly, but in the resigned and weary way of one whose life has asked too much of her.

As you well know, my Lord, I received a tender letter from my mother that Christmas, and each Christmas to follow. She gave many details about the savage girls whom she directed, describing the way in which she bathed one new arrival four times in a row, scrubbing her skin with a soft bristle brush to remove the layer of grease with which the savages covered themselves, and this account did pierce my heart a little. Yet also she enquired anxiously over the state of my soul, and asked whether I went regularly to mass and confession.

But all of this you know, my Lord, for in my sorrow you held me fast to your side.

In each Christmas letter, my mother wrote admiringly to me of your glorious Jesuit martyrs in New France. It would be her dearest wish that I should become a priest, she said, to one day serve you in the Missions in New France. And I began to seek out the Relations of these men, to read of their bravery and their sacrifice in your name and the glorious ends to which you had brought them, and I dreamed of making such adorable sacrifice myself one day. I hoped that in so doing I would be re-united with my mother one day, or even that she might hear of my martyrdom, but you lovingly called her to your side before this could come about, after which, as you know, you withdrew from me, and I suffered a dark night of the soul which lasted many years, so that it was only in my mature age that you gave me the willingness to do *the good that I would but did not*, in the words of St. Augustine. Now my Lord, I know that my mother, your handmaid, does look down on me smilingly, and intercedes for me most willingly, as I have fulfilled her desire that I should enter the priesthood and become what was once called a "green martyr" of the wilderness.

You have never made me regret a celibate life; family and children could only be a hindrance to the works of a green mar-tyr. Even so I have been plagued here by my awkwardness with children and lack of natural affection in their presence, which I believe is intended by you, as you intended that my mother should grow distant from me. The savage children divine a sort of coldness in me, and so they tease me, pinch me and poke my stomach—which, as you know, Lord, has bothered me since the time that my little cousins discovered that poking me in that place would incite a sort of rage. The more I protest the more these little savages laugh, yet I find myself unable to join in their laughter, as if you have made the heart itself form a barrier to this

30

kind of enjoyment. I have sometimes seen my temperament as a failing, but in truth I know you have kept me in your protection for your glorious ends. For some of my mother's acquaintances tried to appeal to her natural affection for me, yet nothing anyone could say (including her son, who strongly objected to losing her!) could sway her in her determination to be well-used by you, according to your purpose.

Yes, all of this you know, my Lord, for you have led me to write these words in order to see your purpose as I look back through my life, a purpose I will reflect upon daily until the *fields and vast palaces of memory* are no longer necessary to me (as they are not necessary to you, to whom all of time is one), until the glorious time when you call me to your side, O Lord, in eternity.

From . . . *the terable captivitie and wonderfull redemption of Sarah Baker*

Second Remove

THE NEXT MORNING, after they had given us leave for the offices of nature, we removed from that encampment and they led us onto the frozen river *Connetecut*. Our captors got some slays they had hid near the strand in their passage south; and we were presently put in harness with a strap passing across the forehead, allowing us to drag them. Constance was given a slay to pull alone and a pack of skins nearly as big as her person and belted with a tumpline; which made me terribly unquiet as she was small and not inured to toil, the snow was thick and the sledge though small was heavy with plunder; nevertheless, as she was ahead on the path, I saw she bore it tolerably well at first.

One woman who had joined us at the foot of the mountain was put in harness with me; she was thick with soft hands and suffered greatly; groaning to God &c.; seeing her difficulty in pulling the load our master moved the straps from our foreheads and gave us each a broad one in the room of it, to wrap round the chest which galled me the more as my milk had come in which was the more discomfort, even making me distempered and feverish; I was not under a good composure of mind, yet the Lord did interpose and I was able to carry on; and with that woman, at least, I kept pace, who was a German. Her name was *Marta*.

In our band there were five or six Frenchmen and other Christian neighbors and their children. Strangely I did not come to know very many of the names. I can not explain the reason save that at first, we were not suffered to talk as our masters feared we should elope. Later in the wilderness the travail was hard and, most days, all our vigor absorbed by it. Perhaps this is not true but as I am unable to conceive another, it will have to do for a reason.

(One of those early days a boy of perhaps ten years of age was crying on the path; when I came upon him there I wanted badly to speak with him; yet my master came upon us, and I could not stop or offer comfort. I am sure my heart was galled long after the boy had dried his tears. In these many hours of silent toil I did think upon discourse itself; that while to be together in silence is a balm, as my silence with Mistress Kimball, yet at other times it is precisely our words that the Lord offers as a comfort. When a common tongue is wanting, or when one is made to be silent, the talk of worldly things appears a grace; yet formerly, before this trial, I sometimes disdained to speak to others, or found their discourse trifling. The boy stayed with our band until we neared *Monreal*; his name was Peter.)

There we marched on the surface of the river, the Indians coming behind as the trail was cut by the one in front, and became easier to tread upon with the increasing numbers who had passed, so they made their burden lighter though they were inured to such travel.

O never in my life had I known such weariness, that when we were suffered to halt, and encamp, verily I felt I had never known what *refreshment* was, before this day, when it was so sorely needed.

As they cleared the snow for a "wigwam"–which, as the reader may know, is a sort of Indian tent, with a skin stretched over–one of their dogs espied a hole in the snow the size of a platter. Here it pounced and we heard the screaks and saw the fur flying, and it was a raccoon hiding; the dog let it go scrambling over the snow, then biting its neck and shaking it again; when it stopped we saw the breath return to the beast, only for the dog to pounce again, and tears came to my eyes, being certain that we too were only suffered to crawl and screak pitifully, our breath to return, before our necks should cruelly be bitten. Having finished its deed the dog, bleeding from its eye, commenced to bury the creature, closing a snowy grave in playful fashion, with its nose, when our master pulled the creature from under the dog, and roasted it, and though the guts were not rinced and the fur attached withal, yet we ate this eagerly as a savory morsel.

There too by that fire we dried our mocasens and leggins and I took Constance's dress and stockings so she stood shivering in her coarse blanket. My night dress I had been suffered to keep and endeavored to dry it upon my own corpse, but the salvages removed their garments and stood naked before us, as animals. They had some skins in the slays, on them we lay together by that fire, the German Marta, Constance by my side and the salvages flanking us; as the fire warmed these beasts, they began to smell terribly. So it was a blessing that most of the journey the cold would quell such a terrible rotting smell. Yet they slept deeply and did not disturb us.

Constance had born her trials well by the grace of the Lord; yet at night, and at rest, she was unquiet, calling now and then, *Mother!* as though I should elope without her knowing. As they did no longer bind us, I permitted her to plait my hair, although it was not my wont, yet I reasoned the task might calm her; I had lost my night cap, and, captivated in the early morning as we were and not given leave to do aught but dress and put on our shoes; so my hair hung, which did provide some warmth for my ears as I wore no cap. It was not my habit formerly to have my head uncoverd as it stirred my vanity; yet here I took no notice as fatigue had overcome me.

Thus, in His mercy the Lord gave me rest. I recall that first the voices of my companions went on for a time, during which I wondered that they had breath to speak.

That German called Marta prattled, for the Indians had taken a punchbowl she owned, a treasure to her, and dashed it against the floor; O, such a punchbowl, she said, and dolefully now listed its qualities, of porcelain was it fashioned, and gilded edges, too, its stand was bronze and molded with leaves and flowers crafted so finely that they looked *alive* (which word made her sob anew), and on the porcelain a scene of great lords at table, drinking punch from the very same bowl upon which was painted the *same* scene exact, and perhaps these little scenes went on for*ever* (she cried out so I feared she would wake our masters and anger them) and how it was fashioned, and in such-a-town and now gone, gone! one thought she cared more for the punch bowl than the poor departed souls she had certainly left behind; though in her fixing on the gilded bowl, its worth in *groats*, the pains taken to ensure it on her sea voyage, wrapped in a goose *doovay* &c. all which she mumbled and muttered and cried softly, these concerns perchance took the room of others much greater and harder to bear; thus the Lord vouchsafed her sensibility, for He works in wonderful and awful and mysterious ways. One of the Frenchmen, whose tongue she spoke, having sympathy for her wailing gave her a bit of jerked meat he had put by and this quieted her finally.

There came to me a picture of my hens, their little house having been fired, roosting fearfully in the trees. And I slept.

Letter of Father Simon René Floquart
respecting the Mission of St. Ignace
at La Rivière des Anges

February, 1704

Reverend Father in Christ,
The Peace of Christ!
Praise the Lord for all is well if He is by!

THE LORD BLESS and deliver our Father Dublon. At the time of my writing he is ill with what we believe is *smallpox*, as we have visited three savages in the past month who have contracted the disease, in order to give them Extreme Unction. So it pleased God to save two souls who had been reluctant! The third, a savage girl, had most willingly been baptized, as the records will show, and was as devout as any savage child can be. To our horror, we found the juggler at her side with fetishes to cure her illness, the fine bones of a green heron and some odd tiny brooms of hair, but after Father Dublon admonished them, they sent him out promptly and we had ample time to administer the rites before her last breath and were assured that her soul was out of peril.

Nevertheless, it has not been easy to make them fully understand the Lord's work and the good we are doing in our wilderness station. Before Father Dublon took ill, we found ourselves in some danger, as a small band of them began to menace us. Father Dublon overheard them concluding that our rites were an evil spell, and had *caused* the death of the three, and one evening they came to the rectory and bound me as I slept. I do not know if they planned to kill me, but as the others found

Father Dublon on his bed and exceedingly distempered, they consulted with each other, then unbound me and left in peace; therefore, the Lord did wonderfully protect us both. Among the savages the sickness seems to have abated, and is certainly not as prevailing with them as it was two years ago, when half of them died of the terrible disease. Yet we pray for Father Dublon, who remains weak.

Although I am well, God be praised, my sleep has been poor since the night of the incident. For this reason I request here a pillow of chintz, because the former one was stolen by one of the savage children and given to one of their dogs to chew upon, for which neither children nor dogs were reprimanded—and then I have nothing to rest my head upon, and furthermore, the pain in my neck upon waking disturbs my prayer and meditation. In fact, two of these pillows would be welcome to me, as I am nearly sixty years of age, and lately become stiff when sitting, and this disturbs my communion with God. To speak frankly, I am tired. I formerly relied on Father Dublon to shoulder some duties requiring felicity with the savage tongue—hearing confessions, settling disputes and so on—but all falls to me since Candlemas, when he took sick, and on many days I suffer from nervous exhaustion which renders me less sanguine about their teasing.

Constance

CLEAVE THYSELF in two. One is the cold one. The other lives inside thee, where the blood is a warm river.

This was a goodly thought. She fashioned it as she marched, and was amazed, for God had preserved the corner pantry in her mind and in it the pewter plates and cups and the stone jug with its ears for handles, and there were many things on the shelves that she could remember. How to stitch in place, to darn. In the parlor, all of the numbers remained. So with each step she drew a number from that shelf, five hundred forty-two, five hundred forty-three, and up to one thousand, a very great number. Then she stepped down from the chair, and began on her catechism which came to her as beads on a string.

She could see the rooms of the house darkly, but when her mind walked closer, to see what had passed there, the others went down the cellar stairs, into the blackness.

Oh, her feet were very cold.

From . . . *the terable captivitie and wonderfull redemption*
of Sarah Baker

Third Remove

THE NEXT DAY from that place they untied their plunder and
marched us from the edge of the forest to the foot of the mountain, a distance of twenty miles or so, where we joined other captivated Christian neighbors and their French and salvage captors
withal; we were given one pair of Indian shoes and Indian leggins
lined with fur in the room of our wet stockings; snow shoes for
our march, and an Indian blanket for a cloak. There our captors
appeared to hold a council and the plunder and captives divided
among them. During which time Constance asked if they would
separate us; I told her again to keep quiet; yet I too was much
exercised in entertaining it but the Lord was merciful.

Mistress Kimball was in a band that diverged from ours, and
her countenance as she was led away alarmed me not a little. I
prayed the Lord would vouchsafe her health and redemption; or,
indeed, that whatever befell her, she would find strength never
to reprove Him.

We were a smaller party now from an hundred to just 12
souls and two masters, and their Indian dogs withal.

The Commonplace Book of John Baker

THE COWS AND sheep bow their heads, eating the spilt grain. This keeps them near while the fences are rent.

The brown cow must be shot, for her bowels have come out. She was a good cow and calved a big calf each spring and gave much milk.

Bless the men who have moved the dead to their winter crypt (my son John among them, also the infant, a boy.) Bless the widow Field who has cleaned my stone house so that it appears itself again.

Still feathers remain, from the rent bed. I find one in a shoe, a bowl, one lighting on an eyebrow. My determination to rid the house of them, prowling from room to room, seems to engender many more in the room by which I began, as in a beteeming of insects; likewise there is a mad futility in my attempt.

Therefore the travail of my book is a godly one, for God has again spared the library and my little book withal; and in the fixing of my mind on the task, I feel His great calm guiding hand.

BEASTS

Per JOHN ROWLAND

For next unto Man are . . . Creatures rankt in dignity, and they were ordained by God to . . . be Fellow-commoners with Man . . . and are obnoxious to the same casualties, and have the same coming into the World, and going out that we have; *For that which befals the Sons of Men befals Beasts, even one thing befals them both, as the one dyeth, so dyeth the other; so that Man hath no preeminence above the Beasts. All go unto one place, all are of the dust, and all return to dust again:* Eccles. 3:19-20.

From the Record of the Missions of the Society of Jesus in
New France in the year 1704;
Mission of St. Ignace at La Rivière des Anges

On this February tenth, 1704, I buried the missionary Father Jean Dublon. He was forty-three years of age.

S. Floquart, missionary

From the *Journal Intime*
of Father Simon René Floquart

THIS EVENING I was brought to tears by the sight of the bare trees on the hill beyond the palisade, their branches so black against the brilliant pink sky. O, the sincerity of these bent arms reaching to Heaven! Lord, do you mean to show me that something is lacking in my own supplication? Perhaps what you feel in me is reservation, rather than insincerity. But I must write of something else, and quickly, as the thought of lighting another candle is wearying to me.

I am alone now and companionless. There is no one with whom I can discuss something very troubling, and close to my heart. I fear for the soul of Father Dublon, for his end was not as I expected it to be. As he struggled to breathe, he called repeatedly for his mother. No, it was not Our Holy Mother, upon whom he called, but *Maman!* as a child might, asking her why he must suffer so, while others simply died in their sleep, and during this feverish ranting he took the Lord's name in vain many times, and called out again and again, *Non! Maman!* Even as I performed the Extreme Unction, his eyes rolled back in his head as if to mock the words.

O, there is peril for every soul who dies in Adam!

(Now I must light another candle.)

These last days I have longed for Father Dublon's replacement to arrive while at the same time, I would prefer my current burden to habituating myself to some unknown person. I am perpetually tired, sleep poorly, wake with my hands in fists, or muttering to myself, having had dreams in which I am trying to make myself understood, and the savages, knitting their brows and claiming not to understand me, engage in all manner of sinful behavior.

The Commonplace Book of John Baker

Per HORTUS SANITATIS, or *The noble lyfe and natures of man of bestes, serpentys, fowles and fisshes that be mostely known*

DELPHIN is a monster of the see & it hath no voyce but it singeth lyke a man.... They love their young very well and yf it fortuned one of ye younges to dye . . . these olde ones wyll burye them deep in the grownd of the sea because othere fisshes sholde not eat this dede delphyn, so well they love their young.

From the *Journal Intime*
of Father Simon René Floquart

A MOOSE STOOD in the river this morning taking long and noisy draughts. Now and then he lifted his heavy head to regard me, standing on the bank. There was such gentleness in this enormous beast, his soft square antlers, his liquid eyes, but when I realized that Père Dublon could no longer be pleased by my description of a moose or any creature ever again, I was overcome with sorrow, and turned away.

When there is no one with whom a man can freely speak his mother tongue, a great loneliness descends. This must be true regardless of one's fluency in any other language, but for me, it is all the more difficult.

I should not have relied so much on Père Dublon to translate, especially where the gospel is concerned. When they don't understand I find myself nearly in tears. Lord, how long must I struggle, before I can speak with them easily? How long must I bear their faces regarding me blankly? For my own mother spoke fluently with her flock in the Huron, and even wrote for them the psalms and taught them to read the gospel in that tongue.

In preparation for the Feast of the Annunciation, I attempted to draw what my words could not relay. First I found a charcoal in Father Dublon's chamber. (It lay on the table beside his hat. A few white hairs still clung to the black felt rim, the sight of which touched me greatly.)

Taking this charcoal, I worked its point on my paper, drawing from memory a painting in Siena, which I thought might be simple enough to convey the idea I wanted—Mary's fear and awe in the presence of the angel Gabriel. I began with the angel himself, his crown with its greenery, the feathered wings with their dots and stripes. The angel leans forward, beckoning, his eyes penetrating (which I could only accomplish by drawing them as narrow slits) and the words reaching from his mouth to Mary's cloak: AVE MARIA GRATIA PLENA DOMINUS TECUM.

The savages laughed heartily at the feathers—from recognition or from my lack of skill, I do not know—but when I began to sketch Our Lady, a hush fell over them, for they knew her by the hood of her garment. I attempted to show her turning from Gabriel by drawing the right shoulder somewhat higher than the left, and yet she must look back toward the angel, tucking her chin under the left shoulder in fear, so this left side should be drawn rather high as well, which, when I attempted it, made it nearly square with the right so that the turning effect of the torso was lost. But the clasp of her hood—even if the hand resembled a claw—seemed to convey fear and reticence.

A quiet state came over me as I worked, and when the sketch was done the savages ran happily to provide their dyes and brushes, so that I might give some yellow tones to the words of Gabriel, and blue to Mary's cloak, and I was so happy in my concentration that I lost track of time, and when I stood back to contemplate the finished product my disappointment was deep, for the result was no match for the tenderness that had coursed through me as I worked, perhaps foolishly imagining myself infused with the spirit of the artist who had rendered the original so beautifully.

But Our Lady was most favorably disposed to intercede, for the savages fell upon the finished image eagerly, their brows knit in imitation of Our Lady's fear, even lifting their shoulders and tucking their chins, taking on the very posture I had failed to capture. Thus the picture did my work for me, and I see that with its help my words are barely needed, and am most gloriously humbled.

As I write this I realize that the bereaved woman was not among them today as I painted. She has not come to Mass since the death of her daughter.

The Commonplace Book of John Baker

WE ARE A poor batch who remain here, our counterforce and those who have escaped captivity. The men are busy with repairs to the outer fences. Reverend Kimball himself has joined them and may deem my work here too worldly, without understanding its nature.

John Hull came to repair the gash in the wooden door of my house, through which blows a cold draught. When I refused, he regarded me strangely. Might I then compile a list of what has been plundered, and compose a letter for the province withal? (As I sit at my desk I seem to be suited for this work, with my ink at the ready.) I am loath to be parted from my higher task yet here I begin the list,

One Feather Bed of large size £20 12s. 4d.
Barn (fired) £200
100 bushells wheat

(Yet the making of such a list is most disquieting.)

UNICORN

Per ALOISIUS CADAMUSTUS
There is a region of the new-found world wherein are found live unicorns; (with one horn which is crooked and not great) having the head of a dragon, and a beard upon the chin, the neck long and stretched out like a serpent's; the rest of the body is like to a hart's, except that the feet, color, and mouth are like a lion's. . . . What is most strange of all other is that he fights with his own

kind (*yea, even with females unto death, except when he burns in lust for procreation*).

From . . . *the terable captivitie and wonderfull redemption of Sarah Baker*

Fourth Remove

ON THE FOURTH day, when the sun was directly above us, the ice rent wherever it was not thick heretofore, which is to say, wherever the current flowed strongly; and our captors were bewildered as they endeavored to find safe passage. We proceeded in serpentine fashion, for though they recalled the conditions of the ice on the passage south, yet in the meantime it had changed, or so we conjectured, as we did not speak their tongue; so it was that, at that time, by the way of finding our right path, one savage fell in at an interval; the others pulled him out in haste to the strand and all of our party made an halt as they warmed him by a large fire they kindled; they allowed us to approach the fire, and as the next day was the Sabbath we were suffered to observe it; this was the most we had refreshed ourselves thus far on our journey, moreover the wind was low and the fire tended withal by our masters. All that Sabbath we were given rest at the side of the river, for our captors called themselves Praying Indians.

Now I will describe the next day's travel, which was both doleful and rather wonderfully peculiar. After our rest we set forward much refreshed but soon again the snow shoes too began to gall my feet terribly; the swollen feet I had (that brought to mind my poor mother with the gout, years ago; for whom, I saw then, I did not have proper sympathy and fellow-feeling) and the accompanying pain, can hardly be described.

Yet this pain was intermitted as the sun shone now clearly on the wide frozen river; the air grew still, and crisp and light; the sky was a sharp blue, and the snow twinkled with the light of this bright sun, and in my light-headedness I imagined this as the twinkling hand of the Lord come down; for now—perhaps because of my refreshment—I could see that any beauty I had known formerly could not exceed that of this vast, white, sparkling land; I felt quite strange withal, for I did not know how *light-heartedness* might enter in the midst of such a trial, save that despair, removing a mote from the eye, allows us to see the world's beauty most clearly, and, still sorrowing, we are bound in all at once. I offer this as a testament to divine providence; that these brief and clear attentions, however rare in our trials, fixed themselves upon my spirit as the very evidencies of His love.

The Commonplace Book of John Baker

Per EDWARD TOPSELL, *The Historie of Four-Footed Beasts and Serpents*

ELEPHANTS lose their ivory teeth every tenth year; when they fall off, they bury and cover them in the earth, pressing them down by sitting upon them . . . and so in short time the grass grows upon them: for, when they are hunted, they know it is for no other cause than their tusks, and so . . . they desire to keep them from men.

Elephants have a wonderful love to their own country, and, although they might be ever so well delighted with divers foods and joys in other places, yet *in memory of their country they send forth tears.*

Four Cows £20 10s.
One Team Horses £15 10s.

From the *Journal Intime*
of Father Simon René Floquart

ALL OF THE grieving woman's relations, who at first sign of her fever, gathered around her bringing her food and blankets, now pay her no heed, as is the custom when one of them falls gravely ill and is likely to die; and indeed they all seemed much astonished that I made the attempt when I came to their longhouse to give her Extreme Unction, though they had seen me do this so recently during the smallpox. Perhaps they also reasoned that I might now fear coming to her, given that the last time I had spoken these words they had bound me in the night! Indeed, my voice trembled, but God gave me strength. Do they understand better now what we do? Most of the time I feel they do. Then one of their superstitions will arise again; for example, their "prayers" to the tree they felled yesterday. They knelt before it somberly and their words seemed to be in praise of the tree itself. Though horrified, I hesitated to scold them. This was certainly a sin born of cowardice.

From ... *the terable captivitie and wonderfull redemption of Sarah Baker*

Fifth Remove

WE CONTINUED several days until the Conetecut joined the *white river.* Here we kept the river going north and west and broke from the others, while the Frenchmen, they said, went directly to Kebec. We were just six now in our band, the Frenchmen departing along with the other women save for Marta and two savages; myself and my Constance; also the crying boy, Peter. Because the Frenchman with whom Marta had parleyed departed with that band, the savages no longer gave her quarter, and though this day she was exceeding distempered she was made to go first in the march, and having to break the snow, she fell in a swoon and Constance and I endeavored to animate her, but in vain; she would not reply and fixed her eye upon the air, which my master perceiving, he delivered a blow to her pate; and left her there in that wilderness, on that great river, with no Christian burial (though they called themselves *praying Indians* as I have wrote).

O reader, you might imagine what sore trials were exercised now upon our spirits. Our companion gone, our feet swollen and bleeding, dear Constance her ears quite froze so as to lose their color; and my nose too, which ran as my eyes, with the cold, now tingled and now itched and now pained most terribly and finally went all together numb. I did not think on my visage for the pain in my feet was great, and Constance her feet too were frozen white, and the pinch of hunger took hold of us; for many days we had no refreshment but broth from one of their bear skins which they boiled.

Again *The sorrows of death gat hold on me I found trouble and sorrow; Then I called the name of the Lord* and committed all to His Providence.

Constance

THEN EVEN IF she looked in the attic the *thing that had passed* that very day was not there.

Her mother removed her shoes.

Oh, she said. For the toes were capped in purple, the color of a ripe plum. The Lord had surely painted them, for the line where the purple cap started, in the middle of the white toes, was very straight. Her mother rubbed the feet in her hands, which did no longer seem to be *her* feet as she did not feel them, and her mother too looked very strange, and she was afraid.

From ... *the terable captivitie and wonderfull redemption*
of Sarah Baker

Sixth Remove

READER, I tell you that certainly God heard our pleas, and had mercy on us, for that very afternoon, He sent a most merciful storm. The snow came heavy and hard and the wind blew so mightily that I was blind as Tobias; if I turned back I could not see the slay I pulled.

Therefore mercifully we must make an halt, though it was yet mid day. We retreated and turning our backs on the wind found our way to the strand, our masters leading us, though they too were bewildered for some time.

Finally by the Lord's good grace a downed tree was found, which, falling against, it broke the wind; we used the branches to clear snow for a shelter and its boughs for a roof, and banked snow for two walls, the tree and snow making a sort of *lean-to*. From there they kindled a fire; we sat quite pinched in hunger being two days without food, and the snow too deep to be dug in or traversed in order to hunt; over the fire they cooked some thing I soon perceived to be the haunch of their dog, which they killed for our repast; though it galled me I ate it, as did Constance, though she did not know what it was we ate.

Snug in our tree-haven with the storm raging about us, all that had happened was given leave to enter my mind, as if the thoughts had been frozen extremities devoid of feeling, now warming to life. My babe, my children, dead, my husband's uncertain fate; my own sore discomforts. Yet, before our tryal, what had been the words of David, of Job, of Daniel, to me? I had merely recited their lamentations and cries with my tongue only; now I knew them by my whole heart.

"Mother," said Constance, "Your face is strange!"

"Then do not look on me," was my reply.

"And your hair!" I had perceived as I trudged that my hair, as it hung about my face, was white as frost. I said to her, when it warms, it will be brown again. Yet we were melted completely, and the hair still white. Too, I was sure, my countenance was much ravaged as she suggested, but here I did not tarry. In former times I was much given to vanity; it surprised me to feel no pinch or protest, only for Constance and her disquiet on my behalf, and I thanked the Lord for delivering me from miscarriage.

We slept the rest of that day, therefore, and into the next, and our bodies much refreshed the next morning when we awoke to the Indians cooking a broth at the fire, the sky clear and cold. Now rested we could travel on more quickly, though I could not enjoin our savage companions to find and bury our poor friend in a Christian manner.

Constance

THEN THE PAIN had gone, but in order to march she must kindly ask her good legs to place the feet for them, for they could no longer feel. She shivered, then was burning hot. God sent the sun along beside her, who broke through the clouds to comfort her, and made the icy trees to sparkle, and this was a comely thought. But she could not hold to comely thoughts, or to the numbers, or to her catechism; she seemed to be dreaming as she walked, and the rooms of the house were empty.

From the Letter of Father Simon René Floquart to the
Reverend Father Superior of the Missions of the Society of
Jesus in New France, Spring 1704

THE PEACE OF the Lord!

Today I received word that a replacement will soon be sent
for Father Dublon. I pray that he will speak the savage tongue
with ease, as it would be of great help to our mission. My fellow
fathers of New France do so excel at learning various tongues
that such gifts seem a requisite for our order, yet I must admit
that I am an exception. (Although in Gorizia, Greek and Hebrew
were used to shed light on the Vulgate, and I became fluent in
these as well as Italian, Slovenian, and German.)

It is no excuse on my part, but I will attempt to describe
more precisely the difficulties presented me here. Where one
might begin to learn any civilized language by memorizing,
for example, a list of nouns and their declensions, in our savage
tongue the noun rarely exists as a separate, substantive entity,
and while the *sounds* may exist to designate an object, they are often not discrete but *buried* within each verb, the verb being most
prominent in the language, a boat that carries all passengers.
One searches in vain for separate nouns, declensions or cases
of nouns, adjectives with which to describe them, or articles to
define, whether they be known or unique, and so on. Thus the
verb, containing so much in itself, including the things we think
of as *noun*, can express too much for the mind to absorb, and the
tongue in its hasty attempt to accommodate all within each *word*,
is impaired in in its expression.

For example, one part we in French might call a verb, *ithkhe*,
or "moving," is the root of a much longer proposition, housing

a noun within it, so that *tahonathahitahkhe'* means "They were road-moving toward this place," or more simply, "They walked down the road." It is difficult to proceed by analogy from this proposition to form others like it; one has great difficulty getting all elements within the new word as one speaks, as the mind doesn't seem to work that quickly; and to translate one's idea from the French is impossible.

Often the object itself is simply denoted by the verb associated with it; for example, for my pen (apart from the magical properties they ascribe to it, which I have described) they say, *iehiatónhkhwa*, or "someone writes with it."

At Babel God confounded the tongues of men, yet did He not also mean for us to *learn* various tongues in order to spread the Gospel, and in order for this to happen, did He not see to it (as Aristotle suggested in his explication of noun and verb, etc.) that the languages of men have a structure and design underlying them, *common to all?* Yet these savage tongues may properly be described as infelicitous, and depart so much from the commonalities that one wonders what God wants with them, if not to chasten us.

Constance

NOW HER FEET were black like the dead man's mushroom, or a tree whose bark was wet with rain. Seeing them the master pulled a pot off the sledge with the plunder, and warmed some water on the fire, and put her feet into it, and still she did not feel them, but her ankles were nicely warm and the master dried her feet and wrapped them and put them to the fire for sleeping.

When, in the morning, she followed her mother for the offices of nature, and told her legs to place her feet, her feet would not move. It was as if she stood on cordwainer's lasts, her two wooden feet bound by the rope that joined them, so that when one went, the other went also, and she fell to the ground.

She was not hurt. Her good elbows had caught her, and God had made the ground soft with snowmelt and dead leaves.

Mother lifted her from the armpits and stood her up. She must walk!

But the feet were not at fault. They had kept count with the numbers and the words of the catechism. They had tried their very best to obey and could not. So her mother carried her to the offices, but when the master saw her mother carrying her, and walked toward them, her mother laid her down and covered her with her own body and begged the master not to kill the girl.

She cleaved herself in two, and was quiet as a hare, only thinking Our Father who art in Heaven, hallowed be thy name, so that she might sit by the right hand of God with the Holy and Exemplary Christian Children.

Instead the master put her onto the sledge with the plunder, and pulled a thick fur over her legs and belted it there, and she rode like this the rest of the days, and sometimes he lifted her up on his shoulders and sometimes he put her on the sledge, and sometimes she caught a glimpse of her mother ahead on the march, and she was suffered to sleep beside her every night.

In those days the hand that fed the girl was not her mother's but her master's, that smelled of bear grease, and lifted meat to her mouth or lifted the pewter bowl with warm and melted snow, and those same hands bandaged the feet again.

From . . . *the terable captivitie and wonderfull redemption of Sarah Baker*

Seventh Remove

WE MARCHED ON many days to reach the lake *Champlayn* and there to ascend; the water was still and the weather warmed enough that they would stay a time to hunt and we kept the same camp for many days which gave us rest and refreshment. Though we were not so cold now, yet we had the restless manner of horses when they sense that the barn is near; *where* were those French who might buy us of the Indians, and finally sell us to the English, which we knew had happened to others before us? Constance had fallen into a fever, and her feet quite bitten with the frost, so here I could nurse her and she might regain her strength. The passing days should have been sweet to me, for our masters provided ample meat and fish and birds of all sorts; these we roasted and we ate as well as our masters. Fain would I recall those last moments that I had in the company of my child. Yet it was God's wish and design that we should part.

From the Relation of What Occurred in the Missions of the Society of Jesus in New France in the Year 1704; Letter of Father Simon René Floquart, of the Mission of St. Ignace at La Rivière des Anges, to the Reverend Father Superior of the Missions of the Society of Jesus in New France at Quebec

MANY OF OUR savages who are firmly converted nonetheless retain a strong belief in their dreams. In fact, when one of them dreams something, it is expected that others will do all they can to realize the dream in waking life; for example, last year, one savage dreamed he married another's wife; the other willingly gave her up to him, to my great dismay—although I have read of similar instances in our Relations. Just as recounted there, our dreamer seemed unhappy to leave his wife, and they stayed a long time in each other's company, both in tears, before declaring themselves as having "parted" (which might not be remarked upon unless one is familiar with the custom, as no man lives in a longhouse with his wife, but instead stays with his mother's family.)

Other incidents are less disturbing and cause only annoyance and I suspect sometimes they invent having dreamed that they own something they covet; for example, when one of them reported to me that he had "dreamed" of sleeping under my duvet; all of the others insisted that I must give it to him, and so I did, for I must tread lightly where superstition is entrenched. The nights here are very cold regardless of the season, and I hope that I might be sent another duvet, for the one they took from me was goose down, and kept me much warmer than my wool blanket, which is all that is left me. (I can not yet bring myself to claim Father Dublon's wool blanket as my own.)

Our latest trial involves a savage woman who last year lost her daughter to smallpox, she having made herself truly sick with mourning, fasting, bathing in cold water at night, etc., and coming down with such a fever that I had gone so far as to administer the Extreme Unction. Imagine my surprise when her husband insisted that the dead girl merely waits for them in the river and will return in the spring, as he has dreamed! How he will manifest her resurrection is a mystery of course, and when I asked him, a strange jumble of words was his response—that a cousin from the south would bring her, that she would come by the river, that she would be traded for the sun (perhaps another way to say "in *spring*"; although for this word, I have only learned one proposition, which we might translate as *leaves-are-leaking-a-little*, which took me almost a year to recognize as a name for that season.) I suspect that the man merely invented the dream for the purposes of bringing his wife out of her mourning stupor, which indeed it has done. If I instruct them too harshly as to the superstitious nature of the dream, she may return to ill-health. Again these are delicate questions as they tamper with the soul.

For my own part, I seek to receive the spirit of the Lord in my heart. My thralldom to comfort of all sorts has greatly diminished, of course, as it cannot help but do when one is faced with the coarseness of life in a wilderness station, yet daily I dwell upon our great martyrs of New France, and feel that I have suffered nothing by comparison, and wonder if my character is simply too weak to properly glorify the Lord.

I confess to overfeeding, though on the festal days one must eat according to the custom. And one must eat, of course. St. Augustine wrote that one can forever banish a concubine; one cannot forever banish nourishment. I imagined before coming to our mission that gluttony would not be possible due to scarcity (as we see in the Relations of early missions in New France) but with each passing year the Lord blesses our crops and increases our abundance, and the savages have taken to bringing me many meals throughout the day (though the sagamité is wholesome, the grease they use for my portion is amplified I think as a token of gratitude); also the savage population has diminished greatly since the smallpox so there is more to share among fewer persons; and our dear sisters the Ursulines are fond of sending delicacies with anyone they find passing in our direction, and they provide us ample food for all of the feast days. They have an abundance of plum trees and make wonderful preserves with this fruit, and the butter from their cows is snow white, and wonderfully rich! When one is otherwise suffering some discomfort (I have recently caught lice again, for example, and they disturb my sleep) one tends to indulge in whatever consolation is at hand. I know I will not conquer this avarice without the strength of the Lord, and I rest in the knowledge that He wills each concupiscence even as He gives strength to overcome it, in His time.

Your Reverence's Very Humble and Obedient Servant in Our Lord,
Father Simon René Floquart SJ

From . . . *the terable captivitie and wonderfull redemption of Sarah Baker*

Eighth Remove

FOR THERE CAME a day of a warm rain, and the *ice* broke, so we must proceed by the banks in its stead, which place we stayed one week, where they engaged in making wooden traps to catch *Beavers*. For though we did not know it yet their camp was near. The next remove led us away from the banks, which diversion made my heart quicken: "Where do we go?" asked Constance, and I answered surely to a Frenchman's house, where father will send our ransom. I comforted her, "God has made them to preserve our lives thus far; He will not quit now."

Constance

MOTHER, SHE asked her, do you sleep?

No, Constance. How otherwise should I answer you.

Mother, when the Frenchman comes will he take us both?

Surely, said her Mother. Sleep now.

But the girl knew from her breathing that her Mother did not sleep.

Will he keep a housecat?

Who? asked her mother.

The Frenchman.

I do not know, Constance, she said. Now try to sleep. And her mother turned away, but the girl knew from her breathing that she did not sleep.

Constance, she said. If we do not. . . .

And her mother turned back to her, and the fire shone on her strange face where her nose had worn open.

If we do not go to the same Frenchman, said her mother, some man might come with a black dress. You must not repeat his words.

Why does a man have a dress?

That is no matter. But do not speak Latin. It is the devil's tongue.

Mother.

Promise me, Constance.

Yes, Mother. But they will not make us part?

Surely.

Surely?

Surely not, Constance, the Good Lord willing, said her mother. Now try to sleep.

The Commonplace Book of John Baker

LAMIA

The poets say that Lamia was a beautiful woman which Jupiter
loved, bringing her out of Lybia into Italy, where he begot upon
her many sons; but Juno, jealous of her husband, destroyed them
as soon as they were born, punishing Lamia also with a restless
estate that she should never be able to sleep but live night and
day in continual mourning, for which occasion *she also steals away
and kills the children of others.* Jupiter, having pity on her, gave her
exemptile eyes that might be taken in and out at her own pleasure, and likewise the power to be transformed into what shape
she wished.

For Shoes shurt and hat £2 12s

From . . . the terable captivitie and wonderfull redemption of Sarah Baker

Ninth Remove

WE REMOVED from the strand and perceived we no longer travelled north but east, and away from the lake, and climbed a small rise that gave upon a path that human snow shoes had imprinted (for the snow was not yet entirely melted though the water ran in the lake and streams). This path led to the summit and as the trees still had no leaves our view was clear, and we could see into the valley below; whereat, at the edge of a tiny stream, we espied an Indian village.

As we descended there came many Indians, rushing to us, exclaiming, prodding and poking, the savage women especially laughing and prattling, rejoicing to see our two masters return safely, and others firing guns, beating little drums, feasting &c. For God had kindled their hearts toward us and we ran no *gawntlett*; for all of their former miscarriages these savage people did feed us well; they had killed a *moose* (which the Reader may know, resembles a large hart, with square antlers.) This meat they roasted and fed us not the offal as formerly but the choice parts, and all ate a great plenty.

During this feast other Christian English came down the path and in the end of their march was Mistress Kimball, brown-skinned in her Indian dress! I rushed to her but, perceiving her to be as stiff as a stranger, and regarding me curiously, said "It is I, Sarah!" At which, her hands flew to her cheeks, and she exclaimed dolefully, "Oh, I did not know you!" Later, when I was taken to the French and given a looking glass, I understood. Verily, my countenance was greatly changed. The flesh surrounding my right nostril had frosted and worn open entirely, so that, on that side only, it resembled the snout of a swine. When I saw this I could understand why the flesh there had galled me so, and also that the Lord had been merciful, for I was better for my ignorance of it by the way.

Yet still I knew, that I had turned from fair to mean in the course of this journey. Again I felt the pinch of vanity, the very pinch that, deep in the wilderness, the Lord had removed from me; and I fell to my knees and prayed for all of my execrable faults, and named all provinces in which, by His Grace, I might improve: self-denial, virtue, weanedness from the world. With Prudence I asked, *do you not find sometimes as if those things were vanquished, which at other times are your perplexity?*

And again I was chastened, for an answer came to my heart that *the hand of God itself* makes us pervious to vanity; He shows us with wordly cares that we are fallen, and sin; that even our thralldom to vanity or comfort, while it persists, is His pleasure.

That evening at the Indian camp, one among us told the others that we would be sold to other Indians, which arrived tomorrow for their *pow wow* (which the Reader may know, is a sort of Indian celebration with much feasting, hooping, hollowing, dancing, &c.). This came to pass; after which we were led to the middle of the village, wherat these Indians were choosing among us, and we did not see any Frenchmen.

The Indians tied us with leashes, with which to lead us, and they began to choose, leading one away here, the other there. O, mother, whispered Constance, do not let us part. And I whispered, pray only that His will be done! (But Reader, we two had borne this sore trial together, had remained fast together; I could not bear the thought.)

The Lord be praised that I never promised her, for they took her hand from mine and tore her from my skirt; her head hung; she looked to me and her eyes full of a terrible fear she looked back; she was eight years of age at that time, my only living child.

I prayed, may my child never repine against God, may she instead know that He chasteneth in Love.

Thereafter she was led one way and I in the other. I was given over to a chapman and taken upon the water, in a *cannoe*, which the reader might know is an Indian *Boat* made of elm bark, which would convey our party to the river called *Rich-loo*, and on to *Chamblee*. (Now though the weather was not yet warm the Indians were naked save for a skin tied about the waist, by a rope as women wear *pockets*, though instead of falling in two pieces to the sides, as pockets, this skin is of one piece, and falls at the front. I wore again my night dress though it was verily a rag.) So we came to the French fort at Chamblee, and I was sold by that Indian master for 700 livres to a Frenchman and taken to Kebec, praying that the dispensation of Providence should return my daughter to the fold, and that I too should be redeemed, yet knowing, in the words of the Reverend Mather, that *my praises must hold proportion with my prayers.*

From the Letter of Father Simon René Floquart to the Reverend Father Superior of the Missions of the Society of Jesus in New France at Quebec, March 1704

Reverend Father in Christ
The Peace of Christ!

I WRITE TO request that a new monstrance be sent as soon as possible, as ours has suddenly disappeared. Not one of our savages will confess to having taken it, and I cannot ask the men, who are hunting. I suspect that one of them became enamored with it or has set out to trade for something with it, removing it from our chapel with bare hands, which is most horrifying to consider. I have questioned them many times but an answer is not forthcoming.

You may suggest that I teach them of the presence of Christ in the Eucharist with my words, which I have done, yet consider that even Father Dublon struggled to explain this clearly in the savage tongue, and we were both anxious for their souls on this account.

I ask you to consider, too, that this was the only object we had here which was wrought in silver gilt. Although by necessity we follow the rule of St. Bernard in his *Apologia ad Guillelmum*, he does *not* write that the ornament of the church itself—its immoderate size and voluptuous decoration—is an obstacle to true devotion and prayer *for everyone equally*. We must consider the case of savage souls, to whom the appeal of beauty is immediate, and a fitting initiation to the true church. When one is in a wilderness station, even modest ornament is, of course, difficult to come by, but these dear savages are well-served with something small, for our surroundings have led them to be impressed by very little, and we must consider the souls who still await baptism who pass through our mission, and for their sakes, make haste. Perhaps a monstrance might be sent with the new priest, whose arrival I await with great anticipation.

In Him for Whom it is Glorious to Suffer,
Father Simon René Floquart

The Commonplace Book of John Baker

GOD BE PRAISED. Deacon Sheldon has written that my wife is alive, and in Kebec, while our daughter is thought to be among the Indians. Oh, she is young and weak, yet the Lord loves the defenseless and will provide for them, as He does for the Whales-Guide....

Per MICHEL EYQUEM, Seigneur de MONTAIGNE

FISHES (Whales-Guide)

It is assuredly beleeved, that the Whale never swimmeth, unlesse she have a little *fish* going before her, as her vantguard, it is in shape like a Gudgeon, and both the Latines and we, call it the *Whales-guide*; for, she doth ever follow him, suffering her selfe, as easily to be led and turned by him, as a ship is directed and turned by a sterne: for requitall of which good turne, whereas all things else, be it beast, fish, or vessell, that comes within the horrible *Chaos* of this monstrous mouth, is presently lost and devoured, this little fish doth safely retire himselfe therin, and there sleepes verie quietly.

This, *Plutarke* witnesseth to have seen in the Iland of *Antycira*.

For Cloathing (put off in the chase):

> For cloath £7 4s
> For Taylor his laybor £6s 5d
> For Stockins 15 shillings

From the *Journal Intime*
of Father Simon René Floquart

I HAVE PRAYED these many weeks for the arrival of the new priest and God has delivered him safely, so that finally I may envision my many duties divided in two, and the more taxing given to this young one. Indeed he is so eager and pink-faced (his hair, a very light red, seems to have lent some of its color to his complexion), that it is hard to believe he has lived more than five years beyond the age of discretion.

The superior informed me that he spoke the same tongue of our savages, having hunted with some of them near Albany for three months before being called to us. This I acknowledged doubtfully due the fact that I can only communicate in a rudimentary fashion after eleven years in our wilderness station! (I hoped that he might come bearing a new monstrance, but my request apparently did not reach the superior in time.)

So it is a wonderful gift of God that this young man, Père de Jouy, does indeed seem to make himself understood, and the savages respond to his words in their tongue with such happiness and it seems to me, relief, as if they had drunk a long draught of water after a dry spell; and his freshness and youth and easy smile endear him to all, immediately.

Jealousy is unavoidable for me, a weak and lamentable sinner, but I can't bring myself to dislike this young man, as he is so able and willing to help me. Even when he is in repose, upon seeing me he leaps to his feet as a happy dog might, ready to do my bidding. Today, I found that he had begun to the chop the wood even before my asking, working quickly, singing as he went, *Il ne parle que du bon Dieu* (not grunting or groaning, which I do from necessity, or working in quiet deliberation as Father Dublon used to do). What does it matter that God has given this young man the key to what remains, to me, a locked door? What harm is my slower intelligence, if I *stray not far from Him, and nourish the wings of charity with the food of solid faith?*

Constance

SHE DID NOT cry, but cleaved herself in two, so that one was in the slough of despond, but the other put her fingers in the leash where it burned her skin, and pulled there, to give her throat the room to breathe, and commanded her heels to walk for her, as her feet could not obey. She forbade her body to swoon. Yet the word, swoon, when she forbade herself to do so, fixed itself upon her, and she was falling, so the other one had been stronger, after all.

Then she was in a deep and colorful dream. A delphin stood in the waves and clutched its dead child, crying O, my babe. Then the delphin was no longer in the sea but dug its child's grave in the fresh water at the edge of a green swamp, ringed with cattails. It was a woman and a delphin and the dream smelt of the fresh water, of pine and sun.

When she awoke she sat in the middle of a boat. The man put water to her lips. So she drank and shivered and he put a skin over her, and fastened it there. Then she slept and grew hot and woke herself with groaning.

A bird sang what-now what-now, what will it be?

Then the song faded and the fever burned up through her body, and when she woke, she sat by a fire, but her body still felt the boat, and was rocking and nodding.

The Commonplace Book of John Baker

AS HE HAS made the Beasts peculiar and various, even so has He made the salvage and the heathen, yet there are dangers in heathen lands, which I cannot help but seek as I read, so that I may pray for her preservation in the face of them. . . .

Per Sir JOHN MANDEVILLE, Knight, in *The voyages and travels of Sir John Mandeville, KNIGHT: wherein is set down the way to the Holy Land, and to Hierusalem: as also to the lands of the Great Caan, and of Prestor John; to India, and divers other countries: together with many and strange marvels therein*

Men pass through *Inde* through many countries by sea, and then they come to the Isle of Hermes . . . and it is so warm there in that Isle that Men's Members hang down to their shanks, for the great dissolving of the body. But men of that country that know better manners do bind them straight, and anoint them with Ointments, made therefore to hold them up, whereby they may live more civilly. In this Island men and women lie all naked in the rivers, from the beginning of the day til it be past noon, and they lie all in the water but the face, for the great heat that is there, and the women be not ashamed for the men.

From the Second Letter of Father Simon René Floquart
to the Reverend Father Superior of the Missions of the
Society of Jesus in New France at Quebec, March 1704

My Reverend Father,
Pax Christi.

A NEW GIRL arrived this week, carried here by one of our savages. As I have not received word from you to expect her, I assume she is part of an exchange of which we will be informed. I have not spoken with her, as she is being nursed back to health after her journey. She is feverish and mostly sleeps, but I will baptize her *sous condition* when she is well and able. If she is indeed an English girl, she will be the only English now in our mission, as your records will show. (You may recall that of the original group of four girls we had here, two were ransomed back to the English last fall and the other two given to the Ursuline Convent. The Englishwoman with them died of smallpox.)

The girl is exceedingly distempered and her right foot is especially alarming in appearance, as the big toe resembles a rotting beet, and all of the toes have turned black where they meet the foot, and are swollen so that one can barely see a separation between them; yet the savages have chewed upon a certain root and applied it as a plaster and assure me that she will walk again soon; they have wonderful remedies here, such as their poultice for my cough last fall; and yet there is some danger in it, as they tell me they have no need of my prayers for her *yet* (as if God is necessary to bring us back to health only when other means have failed!) and perhaps more concerning is the fact that they intend to *requicken* her, giving her the place of their departed daughter.

Two years ago when the smallpox first came to our mission all of the savage children in that family longhouse were lost but one. Sadly that very one is the girl most recently departed, whose mother was extreme in her mourning. The departed daughter was the only one left in her generation to hold the family line (as the line is held by women) and great expectations had been placed upon her.

It seems likely that this new English girl was the one of whom the savage father claimed to dream. This was the way in which the departed daughter would "return" to them, in the spring, as I might have known. Clearly there is superstition in the custom, yet as long the girl will abjure the Calvinistic heresy I won't interfere, as this habit they have of replacing their dead is an old custom for them and a consolation, and may be the more urgent because of the importance of the family line. I am not certain of the extent to which they believe the departed is brought back to life, but certainly the person requickened is a vessel for their affection which has "gone wandering," as it has been related, without a home. As I am due in Montréal for spiritual direction next month perhaps I will receive guidance on the issue.

It was my wish that the young Father de Jouy, being child-like himself and more at ease with children, could be assigned to this new girl, but because repairs need to be made to the palisade fence as well as the chapel, and the savage men will soon leave on the hunt, her spiritual direction has fallen to me. If no one else can be sent for this purpose, I will of course be resigned to it, but as the English will surely attempt to send someone with ransom for her as soon as they can, I must make haste to insinuate myself, and the faith.

To that end, I request a copy of the *Contes* by M. Perrault, to help her learn the French tongue, as well as more toys. (The old ones used by Father Dublon have *mysteriously* disappeared!) I do not have a good idea of what things might amuse the girl, but I will give an example of one such toy that, in the past, proved to endear me to the savages. It was what the English call a "whirly-gig." This is a small top with cords peeking out of both sides and wound in such a way that pulling them makes the contraption spin rapidly. (I recall a Dutch painting in which the Christ child carries a similar contraption, yet it is shaped as a cross, which could serve double purpose.) I brought such a top in my original voyage; the savages gathered round and wondered if there was a small man inside, to make it spin. This little device made them kindly disposed to our mission and to me as a sort of benevolent shaman. In this matter I have continually endeavored to correct them, and they understand better now than formerly, yet there is often some confusion with their primitive notions. (This original toy also *mysteriously* went missing last year, something which encouraged me to revisit my vows and remind myself that I do not call any possession *my own*.) Nevertheless, such contraptions may be helpful at the outset. If further trinkets can be sent, this may likewise fix the favor of the girl upon me, and, by extension, on the faith.

More importantly, we are still waiting for a new monstrance, as the original one mysteriously disappeared, as I have written. I am most anxious for it to be sent along with the other items I have requested here. (A list follows.)

In the participation of your Holy Sacrifices, I remain,
Your very humble servant in our Savior,
Simon René Floquart

Constance

SHE WOKE ON a bench, in a dark tent. Her skin was damp with sweat. Two dogs lay on the floor beside her, whimpering and twitching in their dreams. Other people were there too; they slept on the benches behind and in front and across from her. One of them bent over her feet and spoke to them, and lifted them (she could not feel them) and bent her knees for her, too, as if she were a doll.

She closed her eyes again, for the smoke stung them sharply and made them run with tears. Under the smoke was the smell of the man who lifted her feet. It was rather like clove, and mint. But the smell stayed with her when the man left, so it came from the salve that he had put upon her feet, which she could not feel but saw glistening there, before the feet were swaddled.

The man tucked her under the rug and spooned some porridge in her mouth, and some water withal. Then she slept again. When she opened her eyes, the man was gone. An old woman in a black fur touched her feet with her gnarled hands, and two women hovered beside the old one, with their long braids going down the back. They wore linen leggings with English lace for edging, and English blankets around their shoulders. The taller one leaned in close to her face, and spoke in their tongue, whistling through a missing tooth.

But the man leaned in to her the most. He was not the master, who had paddled the boat, but another, with scars like worms crawling down his shorn head. He peeked under the bandage that swaddled her feet, and whispered to her in the strange tongue, and carried her out for the offices, and showed her where to squat herself.

There in the light of day, she saw that she had been lying in a bark house, made of a giant side-lying tree.

When the man carried her back inside this bark house the sun was shining down in a great beam from a hole in the roof, and this great beam swam with waves and eddies of smoke, and lit the woodpile across from the sleeping benches. The back of the bark house was dim, bluish with smoke, and hung with grasses and shocks of red corn, gourds and squashes.

The man sat her up on the edge of the bench and soaked her feet in a pot warmed over the fire and slathered them again, until they itched, so that the girl bent to to rub them, but when she did this, the man spoke to her softly in his strange tongue and took her hand away and pressed it with both of his hands, as if to still it. Then he took a shell and dipped it into the pot that hung over the fire, and spooned some porridge into her mouth.

After this he took up the baby and sat on his bench and nursed it. So it was not a man, who came to her bench and slathered her feet, but a woman, whose head was shorn.

Her name was Nistenha.

The Commonplace Book of John Baker

ELECTION

I pray for a sign, O Lord, whether you will defeat the enemy and return these loved ones to me, or if it pleases you to chasten me in anger. And if you chasten me, tell me O Lord, what then must I do? For I cannot sleep.

Per REV. WILLIAM BRIDGE, 13 *Sermons, on Psalm* 42.11
You have now lost your comforts and the shining of God's face. Either God has withdrawn Himself for your sin or not; if not for your sin, He will return again, and that quickly too; if for your sin, labour more and more to find it out, and be humbled for it.

Constance

THEN SHE WAS all alone except for the grandmother with her gnarled hands, who slept under her black bear rug. The women and the baby and even the dogs were gone, and the bark house was quiet, but for the hiss of the fire. She could stand up to go to the offices now by herself. The good feet found their way again, without her commanding them.

The fog was very thick. How long had she slept? Many days, she thought, and she wondered if the round white light that shone through the mist was the Sun, or the shadow of the moon. Then the snowy mountains rose up out of the mist, and under them the great dark pines, so that it looked like a picture of heaven there, with the good Sun trying his best now to come through the mist. This meant that the east was in front of her, and on her right hand was the south, from whence they had come.

Mother, when will you come for me. Will you come or will father come.

*To the Honored Court of the province
of the Massachusetts Bay in the English America*

6 March 1703/4

IT IS MY hope that I, together with my similarly afflicted brethren of Hartfield Falls, may prevail upon the Court for the provi-
sions and means to repair the damages we have suffered in the
month called February 1703/4. (A list follows.)

I must explain to the Court that it was deemed insensible
to give chase during the raid on our hamlet as the snow was very
deep, nearly to the knees, and we had but two pairs of snow shoes
between us, this being the smallest of our concerns *before* the time
of attack. A modest village such as ours, at the edge of the wilderness, has not the means to be vigilant in *every matter.*

Now, however, we now aim to *pursue* those who have captivated our own; for this reason I request the expenses for a trader
traveling to Monreal as well as ransom for my daughter, Constance Baker, eight years of age. (I have previously dispensed to
Mr. Sheldon, *without the aid of the Court*, the ransom for my wife.)
Consider the hope we hold, that our dear remaining ones, if it
pleases Divine Providence, may yet be redeemed.

Your Very Humble Servant,
John Baker

Constance

GOD LIFTED THE fog, and the good sun shone. She followed the path to look for the others who had left the bark house. Instead, there was the man in the black dress, who spoke the devil's tongue. But he did not speak Latin, as Mother had warned her.

Bonjour, that was French.

Then, Hello, he said, in English.

Are you a Frenchman?

Oui, yes, I am a Frenchman. I am called Pear, it means, Father.

My mother will come for me, she said, and she did not look at the man so that he could not curse her with his devil's eyes.

Ah! *D'accord.* . . .

And she looked over her shoulder, but he walked around her, in order to look in her face with his evil eyes, and she turned her head again.

Are you the Frenchman who will bring me to her?

Ah, *desolé* . . . I can not know. . . . A Frenchman seeks you?

Will I go to your house? she asked him, and trained her eyes on the ground so that he could not walk around and try to look into them. For Mother had said they would go to a Frenchman's house.

But the man crouched and turned his face up to hers, in order to catch her eyes in his evil way.

My house, he said, it's the church—*l'église*.

Perhaps Mother would find her there, so she went.

From the *Journal Intime*
of Father Simon René Floquart

TODAY THE NEW English girl, having slept for more than
a week and mostly healed of her ague and blisters and bruising,
made her way down the path toward the chapel. She had been
left very nearly alone, the rest of the women and children having
departed to tap the maple trees, except for the old woman they
leave in the longhouse. This "grandmother" is not ill, but very
lame, and does not do much but sleep during the day. She makes
a sagamité perhaps every three days, and does not require more.
I nearly thought, when I saw the girl, that it was the old woman
herself—their height is about the same—hobbling down the path
on her swollen feet, as she resembled a savage, with her leather
tunic. Yet her young face became clear to me—and her hair! It
had not been braided in the savage fashion, surely not combed
for the duration of her march in the wilderness, and formed a
bushy halo around her head, matted as the mane of a wild horse.

What awkwardness—I spoke to her but perhaps she did not
understand my English, and it is difficult to explain my role here
as her spiritual advisor. She observed me so curiously; I don't
think she has seen a priest before.

It is a pity that she should be without a childhood companion, when our mission, just two years ago, before the smallpox,
was filled with a merry crowd of children. Other than the baby
boy in her longhouse, only three children remain. So far they
have kept their distance from her; perhaps because their parents
have decided she should "belong" to the one longhouse, and not
the other, and until she is established there and requickened,
they have been forbidden to mix.

The savage girls are about her size: Catherine, who is club-footed, and Mariâ. These two are always together. Mariâ's face is very much pitted from smallpox, so that it resembles the skin of an orange. The third child, Philippe, is 6 or 7 years of age, and Catherine's brother. He must tie a bandage (the belt of my old soutane!) around his eyes to go out in the day—the daylight hurts his eyes terribly, and he is mostly blind, so the men don't take him hunting with the others. The two girls are kind to him. They braid corn husks into shocks with him and help him in all the savage tasks he is able to do. Yet they are a forsaken-looking crew, grappling their way along the path; which I have never yet thought, only having tenderness for them, but now I see them through the eyes of the new girl, who, I imagine, will find them very strange.

I regret having sent the two English girls to the Ursulines, for this new girl might have spoken easily with them, and felt, in that way, more welcome. But perhaps she will be in earnest need of company now, and in this way I can more quickly win her soul for the Lord.

I showed her the mission chapel, at which she took quite an interest, tipping back her head and studying at length the wooden ribs of the ceiling, which are knotted, and still sporting their bark. This ceiling must resemble the makeshift shelters that the savages use in their travels. For that reason, perhaps, she stared up at it a long time, while I stood silently, not knowing what to say to her, and praying for guidance.

I recalled, as I watched her, my own childhood curiosity when entering any dwelling. I would often pretend to have a call of nature when my mother took me visiting, and she would take me to a back bedroom, where the chamber pot was found, and there I examined the dressing tables with their open jewelry boxes, their bottles of mysterious powders and creams. Or in country visits she took me through a hallway or private chamber to the outhouse, and even that humble structure seemed most mysterious and wonderful. Even at home I would sometimes force a certain novelty by hanging upside down from the edge of a bed or, lying on the floor, imagining that I could walk upon the ceiling, stepping up and over each doorframe, and so on.

But in spite of the girl's interest, and as much as I esteem our little chapel, I regretted that it could not be more impressive for her sake. For the interior smells like the hay used to plug holes from the wind, and not of incense; the little pews are really benches, and fashioned from the same wood that is cut and piled next to the fireplace, and there is a sense of ordinariness that should be transcended in a church.

After fire destroyed the Ursuline convent in 1650, Madame de la Peltrie gave funds from her income for a new church to be constructed, rather than a chapel. Sister Marie de L'Incarnation was critical of this expense, which seemed frivolous to her in a time when supplies were short and the sisters were forced to use their headbands and wimples as bandages! But perhaps Madame de la Peltrie had carefully considered the immediate appeal of beauty to the savage soul, and it must be similar for the soul of an Englishman, or a child.

In the place of worship, the one true church, we must consider this appeal. I believe our old monstrance did, in fact, attract the savages in this way. Its finely wrought little castle of silver gilt, the rose-cut gems embedded in the stem, the sweet-faced gold seraphim peeking out from the base—How terrible, that a savage must have grasped it with bare hands! Yet still there is no word from the superior concerning its replacement.

Constance

THE STARS SHONE through the firehole. God had placed one star very close to the moon, and he made it shine brightly, as the North Star in the French storybook, with its winding road that led to a castle on a hill. She was filled with wonder that the Pear had permitted her to hold the book, and to look at every picture as if it were not wicked to do so. Then perhaps a wicked man such as he would not find it wicked to look at a wicked book. But she did not think he was one of the evil men in the black dresses that mother had spoken of, for he spoke English. And in his house were wooden beams and benches where one could put the things that happened. Perhaps he had placed her there, sitting on a beam in the ceiling, with her legs hanging down. Or behind the woodpile with the chipmunk, who was delightful in his scurrying. The Pear did not have a housecat, for a housecat would kill the chipmunk.

Mother, I found the Frenchman
If you come to find me you must ask for the Pear
When will you come
Will you come or will Father come

Cures and Simples

EVERY DAY THE widow Field brings bread, a trencher of beans and bacon. What use then to light the fire? To warm the body of one who did not defend his own?

Eastman the cooper came. The men have talked among themselves and wondered, why I have not yet repaired the gash in the door. I told him that the cold blowing through it is fit reminder of my fecklessness. The cock protects his hens with his own life. So is man designed by God, and if he does not succeed, he is cast down, is less than nothing.

He asked if he might simply nail a bord over the hole, to which I replied that I might have done this myself, and was not helpless. At these cross words he left, but not before giving me such a look that seemed to say that he found me mad. Indeed there is madness in waiting. Nights have passed and I do not sleep and am worn and weary and search through these many books for the remedy. It may please God that we should heal ourselves, or one another, with the aid of living things over which He has given us dominion (as the elders anointed the sick with oil, James 5). Cf. BEASTS, whence many SIMPLES come.

CF. BULL: With the gall of a Bull, and the white of an Egge, they make an Eye-salve, and so anoynt therewith dissolved in water four days together; but it is thought to be better with Hony and Balsam: and instilled with sweet new Wine into the Ears; it helpeth away the pains of them especially running-mattry Ears, with Womans or Goats milk. It being taken with Hony into the mouth, helpeth the clifts and sores therein; and taken with the Water of new *Coloquintida* and given to a woman in travail, causeth an easie childe-birth.

From the *Journal Intime*
of Father Simon René Floquart

THE SAVAGES returned from the maple grove yesterday, carrying with them an immodest amount of syrup and dried sugar
candy! In spite of their return I found the English girl asleep on
one of the chapel benches again this morning when I prepared
the host. Every night she has left the longhouse to sleep here,
and seems to think she will come to live in my "house." Finally
today the savage mother, coming to Mass, explained to her in
the savage tongue. Of course, the girl could not understand the
words themselves but nevertheless she was downcast, standing
mutely next to the others as they sang the hymns in honor of the
Blessed Sacrament and of Our Lady, not even moving her lips
when the mother gestured for her to sing.

Certainly her English parents have endoctrined her most
cruelly for she has, I believe, never seen an image of Christ in
His glorious suffering, and turns her head away from the cross as
if it might injure her.

The Commonplace Book of John Baker

I GROAN continually to the Lord for the simplest food repels me and I cannot take nourishment. Oh Lord, send me word from Deacon Sheldon who has assured me that soon his passage will be easy.

2nd Corinthians 12:9 And He said unto me, My grace is sufficient for thee: for my strength is made perfect in weakness. Most gladly therefore will I rather glory in my infirmities, that the power of Christ may rest upon me.

MOUSE CURE

Per THOMAS LUPTON, *A thousand notable things of sundrie sorts Whereof some are wonderfull, some strange, some pleasant, diuers necessary, a great sort profitable, and many verie precious.*

A slayne Mouse, rosted or made in powder & drunk at one tyme, doeth perfectly helpe such as cannot holde or keep their water; especially, if it be used three days in this order. (First Booke, fourty)

Dippe a silken thread in the blood of a mouse, and let the patient swallow it that hath the squynancie, or swelling, or pains in the throat, and it will help him. (Fourth Booke, seven)

MOUSE CURES II (Plinie, *Natural History*)

Being eaten by children, they dry up the spittle. The water in which they have been boiled, helps the quinsey. . . . The ashes of the skinne, applied with vinegar, helpe the paines of the head.

From the *Journal Intime*
of Father Simon René Floquart

THE SAVAGES have brought Father de Jouy and me an abundance of candy, in French tins this year instead of the old bark box, which the ants could find so readily. Amber colored and fine-grained, it is of such extraordinary sweetness that it produces a sort of extasy as it melts in the mouth. Instead of putting the tins of the confection on the table of the rectory, they placed one in Father Dublon's chamber (Father de Jouy's chamber, rather—it is difficult to habituate myself to this) and one in mine. As his door was open I could see that his tin was significantly larger than mine, but I told myself that they had put the same portion of candies in each box. Still, I kept returning to the possibility that they had given him more, and told myself that I might simply open *his* tin in order to confirm that *his* amount was the same as *mine*, which words reminded me that I had taken vows not to possess anything. And even if I had not, the idea of possession is mostly foreign to our savages, who share everything with each other as a matter of course. Even their gifts are fashioned after what they think are the French customs, in order to please us. Surely they must have meant for Father de Jouy and me to consume the contents of both tins in whatever fashion we chose, but as soon as this thought came to me, I found myself opening *his* tin and devouring several pieces. Though I am sure they were sweet to me, I can't recall their taste.

When I confessed my sin to Father de Jouy and asked his forgiveness, he put his hand on my shoulder as if to steady himself, and laughed very heartily. Those who are able to dissolve with mirth in such a way do give us, the reticent, a desire to join them. But in my case, the body itself seems to prevent it.

Clearly the matter was trivial to Père de Jouy, which meant that he was not in the grip of the demon greed that held me fast. And in fact this was the case, for I began to lift the lid of his tin daily only to see that he had eaten none of his candies, and seemed to have forgotten their existence, while my own supply dwindled rapidly.

This sort of disquiet used to come upon me when I broke bread with Father Dublon. He ate more slowly than I, and when I had finished I looked on his remaining portion jealously, though we had begun with the same amount. But Father Dublon was in every way so patient and deliberate in his actions! It should not have surprised me that there was no repast during which I did not wait with my bowl clean and my hands wringing in my lap.

Despite his restraint with the maple candies, Père de Jouy eats his meals in the manner of Teresa of Àvila "devouring" her partridge! (It is said that she resembled a wolf as she tore into the bird, and the novices were most scandalized.) As I finish my bowl, Père de Jouy helps himself readily to second and third portions, seeming to say, God has been good enough to give us this food. Why then would we not enjoy it to the fullest? Indeed it appears that all pleasures of life come easily to this young redhead, which makes it easy to be in his presence. Perhaps the Lord means to give me a reprieve from the jealous manner in which I had been feeding with Father Dublon.

But my mind cannot rest there. Does Père de Jouy simply dislike maple candy? I can't bring myself to ask him, and yet I wonder and brood on this question, and so remain both hungry and well-fed, though I well know that in my *starved mind I lick shadows*, in the words of St. Augustine. What I hunger for is the Holy Spirit, who is with me in abundance, who keeps my tin overflowing, so that there is never need to doubt Him or worry about His dwindling.

In my fixation on the candy I seem to have forgotten my young English charge. Surely I might give her some of the candy from my own tin, perhaps one after each lesson, to associate that kind of learning with sweetness. The catechism goes terribly still, for what is a catechism if *I* am the one both questioning and answering? How much she hears and retains, I do not know, but she will not repeat it. (There is some stubbornness in her character, I think, because her yellow lion's mane is still not combed or braided, although her savage mother would not insist if she resisted even a little, I think.) Yet already she speaks a little French! Her favorite tale is that of Little Thumbkin, who rides in the ears of his parents, which I know only because she somberly commands "encore" when I have finished, her eyes glazed in a sort of trance. I do repeat it when she asks (and many times, too, as she does not seem to tire of it) giving the little Thumbkin a high voice, because the first time I did so, she smiled at that. Oddly the idea of giving the candy to her does not disturb me as it might were I to give it over to Father de Jouy. Perhaps one piece each day would be fitting.

Constance

THE TWO AUNTS greased her hair and combed it very gently, so that she did not fear that they would make her cry. Then Nistenha combed through her itching scalp, and when she found a louse she ate it, or she cursed it and threw it on the fire, as she had thrown the black bark of the girl's feet on the fire, and cursed it. But the aunts with their braids and English lace also called themselves Nistenha. They spoke to her in that tongue, which was not Latin. They spoke as if she understood them, but she did not understand.

Although she understood *érhar*, dog. She loved the dogs. As she lay on her bench she turned her face so that they might lick the grease from it and breathe into her ear, and when they did this, she remembered them. But this could not be so.

Then the aunts with their leggings and lace would laugh, and shoo the dogs away from her.

She lay on her bench and God sent the clouds running across the firehole like a white river, and the moon cut a circle for himself to shine through it, ringed in gold and pink.

Mother, if I sing the words in Latin, but do not understand them, will it harm me?

I hope it will not harm me.

Will you come or will Father come.

She did not see Father's face, but his back as it rounded at his desk, in the study where he made his book. She remembered the book and the study kept him well in her mind. If Father came for her, he would tell them, here is my daughter, to whom scripture is more dear than her appointed food, may she now keep my book with its wonderful pictures and regard it whenever she pleases, and there she would see dragons spreading their wings of silver and blue and breathing pink fire, and her Mother would say, If it please you, O Constance, my child, the gib-cat may live in the garrison house forevermore, and sit upon your lap with its delightful purring. These were goodly thoughts and made her happy. But though she clearly saw Mother's blue dress with its frayed hem, and the pockets tied round her waist, she remembered her face before the cold time, when they had marched, but not the very strange face, which had worn away on one side, for there had been no house and no shelf in that wilderness, where she might put it.

The Commonplace Book of John Baker

DOWNCAST, O LORD. I am downcast.

For I assemble this book in order to commit to memory all that is contained within it, yet today I made what I esteemed a new entry, and, searching the indices, I found instead, it was something I had already written here! At other times, what I have set down looks as strange as if another hand had written it! If I have written a thing, and comprehended it, in order to write it, does something of it not remain within the brain and the body? Is it not living there, not inert, but vital, as humors course through the body without our knowing exactly where and in what fashion, yet subtly we feel them? Perhaps forgotten things have life of their own, moving and gathering force, as a loon who swims under a lake, then bobs suddenly to the surface on the other side of it, calling out in his mysterious voice.

MEMORY (Per RENÉ DECARTES, Frenchman)

When the will wants to remember something it causes the pineal gland . . . to thrust spirits toward different parts of the brain, until they come across that part where it finds the traces left there by the object it wants to remember. . . . Thus the spirits, coming into contact with these pores, enter into them more easily than into the others, by which means they excite a particular movement in the gland, which represents the same objects to the soul and causes it to know that this is what it wanted to remember.

(Per SIMEON SETHI)

The gall of a Partridge, annoynted once a month on the . . . temples of the heade, so that it may penetrate and sincke in, doth profite very much for the confirming of the memory.

From . . . *the terable captivitie and wonderfull redemption*
of Sarah Baker

AFTER SEVERAL months with the Frenchman, I was redeemed, along with three other English women and one English
boy. The reader can imagine the sorrow bound up with the joy
of my release, when my Constance was not among the others in
our band. Deacon Sheldon assured me that another means could
soon be found for her redemption, and I put my trust in the
Lord, and by His grace was soon returned to my husband and
master, who had become most ill in his disquiet.

As the ground was no longer frozen, upon my return were
buried the fallen of our hamlet, among them my son John and
the baby Ezariah.

Having been well fed by my Frenchman, my health was
more robust than my husband's, and I nursed him and he recov-
ered his health, yet as he suffered the pangs of regret from that
dark and terrible day, and on behalf of our daughter, and I did
not find him altogether sound in mind.

From What was Exchanged between his Excellency Joseph Dudley Esqr. Capn. Gen & Gov in Chief of her Majesties Province of the Massachusetts Bay &c. and The High and Mighty Seigneur Phillippe de Rigaud, Marquis de Vaudreuil, Chevalier de l'Ordre Militaire de St. Louis and Governor General of New France

Sir,

I am most exercised at the intimation that your Excellency is unwilling to withdraw our English captivated by your Barbarians. As you must know, Half of these Christians are children, and their parents most sorrowful and distressed. This alone should cause you to reconsider your position and return them to us.

I eagerly await your reply.

Your Vry Hmbl Srvt
Joseph Dudley, Esq.

Constance

EACH DAY THEY went to the Pear's house first, to speak in Latin, and to sing.

She loved the songs. She did not understand the wicked words, and did not sing them, and if they were beautiful, then perhaps the Lord had sent them to her as a consolation, until her mother would come, or her father would come. For watching her, He sent many other consolations, such as the trees with golden teardrops on their bark, and the otter who delighted in his swimming.

And each day when the Latin was done, the Pear gave her a maple candy, and read to her from the beautiful book. She loved the book. For in it an old woman, who was truly a fairy, told a very good girl that for each word she said, a flower or a precious stone would fall from her mouth, but the wicked sister shed a toad and two snakes when she tried to speak. The French words of the story were like the beautiful flowers and precious stones: pierre, fleur, fille, fée.

Then Pear recited again in Latin, and asked her to say the words, but she willed her mind to make of the Latin words the toads and snakes and nonsense, and this was simple, for there were no pictures in that book.

Then she would return to the bark house. If there were no nets to weave, they lay on the benches and were wickedly idle. The other children played outside with the dogs or with a little catapult made of an English spoon, and they launched pebbles from it, and ran to measure how far the pebbles had sailed, and she wanted to go to them, but Nistenha took her arm, and pulled her back.

So she watched them from a distance. The boy wore a black bandage on his eyes and the girls led him along the path and they played a game with some painted plum seeds, still he kept on the bandage and the girls told him what side of the plum seed to turn, and the dogs went out to them and licked them as they sat upon the grass, where the deer had pressed it down.

She had sat there before on the grass where they were. The dogs had licked her face, and she had thought of many moments and minutes that she would not remember, being there on the grass with the dogs. But she did not know, having come there when she did, how this could be so, except that she had been in a fever, and dreaming.

From the *Journal Intime*
of Father Simon René Floquart

GLORIOUS TIME of fresh wind before mosquitos, may the
Lord be praised! The people start their planting, and flowers
with purple cones, yellow-cups, pink-petals, spring up along the
path; the sun pulses warmly on the river. How the eye stirs to life
with this varied palette! How the body melts out of its winter
contraction!

There is word today that a trader comes with ransom for the
English girl. Governor Vaudreuil has sent orders that we must
hear him out and the savage parents consider his offer; this much
he has promised the English Governor Dudley. But what the
trader will offer for the girl is still unknown.

Just yesterday the girl asked, Where is my mother? in English, and, when my answer did not satisfy, in French. It would not
do to point out that the Indian who has adopted her also calls
herself her mother, and as I am trying to gain the girl's trust, I
am loath to disappoint her; therefore, I answered that I do not
know her parents' whereabouts or plans for her, which, until today, has been true.

Mais, elle est où ma mère? These words, spoken just as a little
French child would speak them, felt so familiar to me that I was
taken aback. Then I remembered that these words had been spoken by a little animal in the *Contes* we had just finished reading.
And then as the girl repeated them in a more imperious tone,
they struck my heart most terribly.

In fact, her question had once been my own, when my
mother took me to stay with my aunt "for a time." I cried bit-
terly, for I knew it would be longer than *a time*, and that same

night, I eloped and ran home (having overheard that my mother had not yet left for the convent but was only still making her preparations) and clung to my mother's ankle like a fetter, and although she did not beat me, she only shook her head, and said *mon pauvre fils* with true indifference, which the Lord had given her so that she might part easily with me. Of course, I was returned promptly to my aunt. I have not thought on it for these many years, for I was old enough, and knew better than to show such weakness.

Though she did not encourage me with affection, still my mother was made to say those words, "my poor son," and return me *several times* to my aunt's house, in fact, until her departure, by which time my own heart too had dulled, as an infant will sometimes tire from its screaming and quiet itself. In this way, my Lord, I am reminded that you give detachment to us as a gift, as our affections are so often immoderate, and cloud our true purpose on this earth!

The Commonplace Book of John Baker

Spots (remedie)

The blood of a white hen, on a freckled or spotted face and thereon suffered to dry, and afterward wiped away, clearelye take away all spots from the same. *Mizaldus* had this from a certaine Italian.

Letter of Father Simon René Floquart to
the Reverend Father Superior of the Missions of the
Society of Jesus in New France

I RECENTLY met with a trader dispatched by the English Governor Dudley and his officers to procure the English girl delivered to our mission this spring. When I told the savage mother that the trader was here, she was quite exercised, speaking harshly to me, although I assured her that the governor Vaudreuil had only asked us to hear the man out, and that he had made no agreement for her return with the English, only that she would consider whether the man offered anything for which the girl might be traded. Yet I sensed that the adoptive mother was reluctant, and this allowed me some hope.

The girl ran ahead on the path, her excitement perhaps blunting the pain in her feet, for I had tried to tell her in English that someone came "bearing a message from your parents." I came along slowly as is my habit, and the savage mother kept pace with me because she was, with the prospect of losing the girl, heavy of heart. Father de Jouy met us at the rectory to translate, and there we fed the trader, who explained that he had spent the funds for a ransom on the way, and upon reaching us had no money to buy her of the Indian who owns her, and no other girl to offer in her stead. Of course, the savage woman then denied to return the girl, and after Father de Jouy had translated her denial, the girl ran out of the meetinghouse.

The English trader himself was thin with worn shoes and as I have said, clothed in rags. Indeed it was only by the Christian Charity of our mission that this Boston infidel did not starve to death, for only the girl's father had paid him, and that so poorly that he had incurred debts along the way; the English had arranged the meeting, it seemed, but had given little charity of their own.

Happy was the trader to sup with me, and he devoured a bowl of sagamité that would feed half of our mission, explaining all the while why the English disdain missions such as ours, and indeed any charity or good works. In short, as we know, their belief in the divine election and predestination of a few serve as an excuse for all to behave in whatever way they will, and many English indulge in spirits and excite the savage women to incontinence, to which they are not naturally inclined.

Informasen to Mr. Sheldon to be givn to Jon Bakur of Hartferd Hils

I am hom yeter Day from oke fort. I espyed the gurl, Constans (Jon Bakur his doguhter) & spok to hur & ye Indian her mster at oke fort & I Ham afrad the Indian would not let the gurl go. I wesh you wood be so Cind as to previde the dets I acrud, but heve not incerted them by reeson I cant make up the accts til I return from candeda. I wesh Hartely we had got her bak & I Ham Hartely sorey. Poraps in her sted an Idnian gurl can bee traded or poraps Mistr. Sheldon or The gurls father may convins hur betr then I Ham able too.

Joseph Hicksen

Constance

SHE LAY ON her bench and cried immoderately, and did not mind that she would be beaten, for the wicked one inside of her was most angry.

A word from your mother or father, the Pear had said. But her mother had not come and her father had not come.

Do not speak Latin, Mother had said, the language of the devil. This was the Pear! With his *robe noire* he was the devil *vraiment*, and she would punish him. She would not speak to him, and when he offered her the maple candy she would close her mouth, and when he read to her from the story book she would cover her ears, and refuse him forevermore!

Then Nistenha entered the bark house and beckoned to the field, saying *Ha' o ki wà hi*, come on then, for they were going to the fields to pull the green shoots on their planted mounds. But the girl could not answer her! She did not speak their tongue!

Yet she knew *jaghte oghte*, maybe not. This was their way to say *non*.

After she said it, she closed her eyes and waited for her beating.

It grew quiet in the bark house. The pot hissed on its crane over the fire.

When she opened her eyes, they had gone. Outside, the children of the other bark house were playing with their catapult again, the boy with the eye bandage and the girls Pear called Catherine and Mariâ.

She was forbidden to talk to them. She did not know why, only that the aunts and the grandmother and Nistenha drew her away when she approached them. Now she would not heed them, for she was angry and wicked. And suddenly, too, she knew what she might do with the catapult.

She did not know how to ask for it in their tongue. Yet if she asked, they would give it to her, for it seemed that nothing in this place belonged to any one of them. So she went to them and put out her hand, and the one called Catherine put the catapult in it, and she took it, and put it under her sleeping bench.

Then she sat by the burr oak tree with its low spreading branches and was immoderately sorrowful, and the children, who had gone inside their bark house, peered out to see her crying there, but they did not ask her to return the catapult.

She lay on the ground and slept, and when she woke God had painted the sky brightly orange and pink, and the frogs were singing, for he knew she loved to hear them, and was sorry for her tears.

It was the time that Nistenha and the aunts and the baby and the grandmother would go to the chapel with the wicked Pear, and the children and aunts of the other bark house would go also.

Soon she heard their Latin words join the song of the frogs. The song was most soft and comely, for all of its wickedness.

When they returned Nistenha held out the bowl of sagamité, and said *wakotà*, I receive it. But she would not receive the bowl! So she refused to repeat as Nistenha wanted, saying *jaghte oghte*, maybe not.

From . . . *the terable captivitie and wonderfull redemption of Sarah Baker*

THEN ALTHOUGH my husband ate again, he neglected the tasks of men in order to sit at his table, and complete his book, which, although there were a few verses within, concerned itself mostly with worldly matters, which was the more disturbing to me.

I often heard him speaking aloud at his desk, though he was alone in that room. He told me that he spoke to God, who wished him to complete the book before the infidels returned.

There was much need of restoration in our hamlet, which might have restored the blood to his face withal. Fences rent, houses fired or chopped, our front door which let in the cold, and which he suffered me to stuff with wool but would not permit any one to nail even a board over it, for it served to chastise him (this I thought) for that dark day on which he failed to save us. Yet the sin he committed, dear reader, was in believing that he could have saved us, if our salvation Providence had not decreed.

Reader, when my husband showed me the book I was unquiet, as it grew exceeding strange, as did his mind, and contained unholy predictions &c.

Natural-predictive significations of the body: Physiognomie, chiromancie, metoposcopie &c.

CHIROMANCIE

1. When there are four lines in the hand-wrist all alike, and well-coloured they signifie to him that hath them, that he shall live eighty or an hundred years.

15. A circle near the Line of Life, he loseth one eye; if two, he loseth both.

16. Lines from the arm to the wrist, not joyned in the end, but beholding themselves oblique signifies *a man shall inhabit out of his natural country, and shall die there*; and by how much greater they are found in the beginning, the sooner; and the bigger they are in the end, so much the longer ere he die.

From the *Journal Intime*
of Father Simon René Floquart

THIS MORNING the English girl arrived for the Mass and stood mutely beside her adoptive mother (who had begun the prayers), her head hanging. I felt deep pangs of sadness as I withdrew to say my orison, and when the Mass had begun, found myself in tears at the sound of their voices raised together. (The English girl did not sing, however.) I am often moved during the Mass by affectionate awe, or by the success of our mission, but I suspected that these tears were different, and resolved to examine their provenance after Mass.

I was about to sit under the large oak tree in lectio divina, when I walked through a web that had been spun from my tree to the one opposite it on the path. (These little spiders love to weave their homes in precarious places. The many webs up and down the path are wonderful to behold when the morning light comes through them, and the dew shines there like little jewels.) As I stood brushing off my soutane, I felt a pinch on my leg. A hornet, I thought. (For I had marvelled at the grey nest clinging to the oak all through the winter, its layers as light and fine as a pastry's.)

And then another pinch, more painful! I turned about in panic, recalling the nightmare in which I am ambushed by the Hurons on this very path. Yet another sting—this one, I perceived, caused by a small stone—and I cried out, only to notice the English girl hiding behind the tree opposite my oak. She shot these stones from a tiny catapult fashioned from a French spoon, bound by leather to some twigs!

Arrête! I cried, then in English, Stop!—but as I bent to confiscate the weapon, another stone hit my cheek and stunned me, so that I stood doubled over on the path, holding my face. At this the girl dropped the contraption and came out from her hiding place and picked up my book, which had fallen, (the nuptial poetry of St. John of the Cross) and handed it to me, and we stood there, out of breath, and exchanged a few words—*désolée*, sorry, *ça va, ma fille*, etc.

I turned my face to the girl so that she might see what she had done, for a little blood oozed where the stone had hit my cheek. I felt as I had when as a child my cousins played roughly with me and what stung was not the wound but my unfulfilled wish for their solicitude.

Why was she angry? (I remembered then, I had once taken a pair of scissors and poked a hole in my aunt's stocking and had taken pleasure in her interjections when she discovered it, perhaps because I had *moved* her in some way—which felt something like a kindling of affection!) So I stood bleeding, tearful, panting slightly, beside the girl, not knowing whether to reprimand her or to tell her that I too had once been lonely, and had missed my mother. More than this, my young soul had felt that *all was lost* if my mother was lost; I had not known how to proceed; I had not *wanted* to proceed. But in fact He had *not* taken all, had provided me shelter, food enough to live, and *affection enough* to sustain myself.

Before I could speak these words, I observed a leaf suspended in mid-air before us, just in the middle of the path. The girl had seen it too, and as we looked on, the "leaf" grew appendages, making rapid motions with them in order to move along the one filament that was left of its former web, then gathering, casting and darning with all the knowledge that God had planted in its soul. For He does not apportion despair to His lesser creatures, so that we might observe them and take our inspiration. So Father Dublon and I observed last spring when the great storm uprooted the tree with the eagles' nest, and while the sky was still rumbling they set to work in the neighboring tree, and the branches they lifted in their talons were as tall as any man. Yes, *as God labors and works in all the creatures on the face of the earth, all things are possible* (St. Ignatius), so they persisted. So the Lord made the girl observe this before I found the *words* to explain it to her.

And had He not given this very spirit to the savages here, after the smallpox? Did the blind Philippe, and Mariå and Catherine not laugh as they shelled the dried corn, or played their game with painted plum seeds, or hobbled together on the path to the river? Did the savages not continue their comings and goings, from chapel to the field or the hunt, and back to chapel, as if they had never been sadly diminished?

Constance

ALL THAT NEXT day the girl was idle, and anger and wickedness burned within her. When the others came back from the chapel and the field, Nistenha passed her the mush but she refused it, and passed the bowl to the aunt with her whistling tooth.

Nistenha was not angry, but passed another bowl to the girl, with a shell spoon inside it, and spoke something that she did not understand, for it was in their tongue.

Yet Nistenha spoke these words so gently that the very gentleness made the wicked one inside the girl boil with anger, and she grabbed the shell spoon and threw it against the iron pot, where it cracked and fell into the ashes.

She cleaved herself in two, and one was a hare and made no noise, but trembled. For surely they would beat her very soundly now for all of her wickedness. The fire hissed and a burning smell rose from the mush on the cracked shell-spoon.

Nistenha left the bark house. When she returned, her hand curled around the switch.

But it was not in fact a switch, rather something small, which fit in her hand.

Then with her head downcast, the girl perceived another bowl in front of her, but this bowl had a silver spoon in it, an English spoon.

Now Nistenha held the bowl in front of the girl, and God sent the sun through the firehole, and lit the handle of the spoon so that it gleamed in its wooden bowl.

Suddenly she was very hungry, for all day and the day before she had refused to eat, and she took the bowl and ate it greedily.

The mush was warm and the wicked part of her quieted as she ate, and when she was done she yawned most grandly. She lay on her bench with her feet to the fire and Nistenha pulled the bear skin over her.

Then the girl looked up at the beam of light, swirling with smoke, and was filled with wonder. Although she had disobeyed, they had given her this silver spoon, as a gift, as if to please her. She felt the warmth of the fire, and the pulse in her good feet, and remembered that when the black bark had been lifted from her feet, her skin had been so new underneath, and so pink that it had looked like the skin of another, who was not quite Constance any longer.

This was a troubling thought.

That night she dreamed that she stood in a field planted with mounds of yellow corn, and the squash with its leaves round the mounds, as a skirt, and the green beans climbing up.

The people of the bark houses came to her. Over and over they spoke the same word, but she did not understand the word they spoke, for she did not speak their tongue.

What must I do, she asked them, to have the blessing? For only then would she understand the word they spoke to her.

And Nistenha said: The blessing has been earned, and has come before you. Then she took a fish and buried it at the base of the mound and said the word again, *Skentsiese*, new fish.

Then the girl understood the word, which was her name.

The Commonplace Book of John Baker

METOPOSCOPIE

Per RICHARD SANDERS, Student in the Divine and Celestial Sciences, his *Physiognomie and Chiromancie, Metoposcopie, The Symmetrical Proportions and Signal MOLES of the BODY, fully and accurately handled; with their Natural-Predictive Significations, etc.*

THIS POSITION of the forehead lines renders the person to be disposed to divers things, having a various genius and a flattering, false, unstable fortune.

Such a line of Saturn in the forehead, with the line of Jupiter denotes the person shall suffer much prejudice by lands and possessions

Sarah (on a *loose leaf*)

My Dear Daughter,

I have mended and refilled the mattress and we are nearly finished with a quilt sewn from the clothes of the dear departed here, and will start on a braided rug from the same. ~~their little clothes~~ It rains daily and spring comes early. I have seen mayapples in the glen. They are large and the white flowers showing under the leaves. The creek at the bottom of the hill is four feet wide. You would jump across it, and come home with wet shoes, and dripping. I should not be angry at such antics now, my heart should gladden to hear you, to hear my children. All these familar sounds of spring are oddly quiet to me, there being no children to run about in its warmth. Although the others nearby do have children, hearing them does not

Constance

FOR ONE MORE day she did not go to the fields, *jaghte oghte*, but when she thought of the baby on his cradleboard she wished to go to him and take him down from where they hung him on the tree, and squeeze him and coo to him with much cherishing.

The word was strange. *Cherishing*. Perhaps it meant *affection*. No, this was not the right word, but something rather like it.

Then it seemed the English words had gone into another room in the English house where her mind did not want to go, but she would not dwell upon it. For she loved the baby! And this was strange. It was a thing she had thought before, in the English time.

So she went to the tree at the edge of the field where they worked and brought the baby down and unbound him from his board, and set his little feet on the ground. Kneeling there she opened her arms to him, and he marched to her with knees high, in weaving steps, shrieking with pride. This was most delightful.

Then he wanted to step up the stone and let himself back down again, searching for the ground with his toe, so she permitted him, and picked him up when he fell, and carried him down their rows to watch the planting.

The next morning she followed the people to the fields again, and the other children came to her, speaking their tongue though she did not understand it. Now Nistenha did not draw her back from them. Mariâ and Catherine led her to the tall grass to hide from Philippe and whistle so that he would find them, and then she and Mariâ were the ones who hid, and

Catherine and Mariâ showed her that her hair must go as theirs did, in two braids down her back, so they plaited it.

After this they spun and spun to make themselves dizzy, and fell down laughing, and she was full of wonder that these children also went nonsensing. While she spun she said the English words, out of his mere good pleasure pleasure pleasure, so they said it too, although they did not understand the words.

Nor had she truly understood when she had learned them in the English time.

Quest-ce-que ça veut dire? They asked her. But she did not know the word, pleasure, in French, or in their tongue. Only that in English it was rather like delight. This was strange, for she had not thought of delight when she put the beads of her catechism onto their string.

When their play was done and she came back to Nistenha, and the tall aunt and the short aunt with the missing tooth who were also called Nistenha, and the grandmother, they did not scold her for playing. She followed along behind Nistenha and took seeds from her basket and pushed them in, and smoothed the dirt over as she saw them doing. In the fields they sang as they worked and sometimes they talked in their tongue. But still she did not know their tongue. To her it was like the buzzing of bees.

From . . . *the terable captivitie and wonderfull redemption
of Sarah Baker*

THEN IMAGINE our dismay to hear that the English trader
could not redeem my daughter, because the evil Indian parents
would not let her go. O Constance (I spoke to the air) Let thy
fear be thy confidence, and the uprightness of thy ways thy hope!

Reverend Kimball preached of the little maid, brought *captive* out of Israel, who waited on Na'aman's wife, and said unto
her, "would God my Lord were with the prophet that is in Sa-
maria, for he would cure him of his leprosy" and he assured us,
the little maid did not forget Eli'sha the prophet, and his Lord,
the God of Israel. Her words were His, and made Na'aman to
believe, and to renounce the rivers of Damascus.

From the *Journal Intime* of Father Simon René Floquart

HAVING WITHSTOOD the rude attempts of the English trader to recover her, the little English girl is nearly always with her new mother, first planting, and then weeding in the early morning and late afternoons. She carries the small boy on her hip and coos to him and talks to him, even now a little in the savage tongue. In her affection I am reminded that Christ Himself came to us as an infant, in a sweet innocence of pure and glowing light.

The girl is eager to see me, and friendly, but when we study her catechism she repeats the words at a whisper, which I cannot hear in order to determine if they are correct, so that there is still an unwillingness in her demeanor that troubles me. Once she is together with the others in Mass, she refuses to recite even what I have taught her; I cannot imagine how we might eventually persuade her to properly receive the Host. I cannot reprimand her, for the savage parents are so gentle with their children, and I must not seem harsh in comparison.

Always in Mass when she sees me crossing myself, she squeezes her eyes shut tightly. Again and again she has done this, even puffing out her cheeks as if to hold her breath during the recitation of the psalms.

Constance

THEY DID NOT show her their ways of doing things, as Mother had shown her to throw the boat through the treadle, to darn, to press the cider.

When they made their baskets, she could pound around the wood and loosen its bark, and peel away the bark with the knife in thin strips, but the strips would not bend for her to weave them, and flew open. When she finished her basket it was not fast, and the corn fell through it to the ground. Then they gave her basket to the baby.

Next the tall aunt gave her a needle and thread, and held out her linen trousers, so the girl stitched neatly where the trousers had rent, as her Mother had shown her in the English time.

Likewise they gave her a knife, and hung the deer from a low branch so that she could reach it. So she pressed the knife into the skin above its belly, and pulled, as if ripping a seam, and the people gathered the steaming insides into their buckets.

She was filled with wonder, for in the cold wilderness she had felt inside her skin the same great steaming warmth, and with it God's good mystery, now blooming out so that it was everywhere at once.

From . . . *the terable captivitie and wonderfull redemption of Sarah Baker*

READER, I confess that I was not entirely sound of mind myself, and would steal a loose leaf from my husband's table, though they came very dear, and compose a letter to my daughter, though I had no currier and no means of sending it.

Constance

HIS NAME WAS Philippe, but Nistenha called him *Aukwehtá:ku*, grey squirrel. He helped her to flesh the deer hide over a beam, to press the bone into the hide and scrape it clean of the fat that wobbled under its pearly membrane. She took the bone down from the corner pantry of her mind, for it was very like a rolling pin in her hands, and the fat like a dough that she rolled evenly forward. When her hands tired, the boy took the bone from her, and fleshed the hide.

The boy wore his black hair to his shoulders. His smooth skin shone with eel fat. He was shorter than she was, but old enough to go with the men, as the other boys did. But he did not go with them because he could not see in order to hunt. This is what she thought, but she did not know their tongue, so he could not tell her.

Here, it did not matter that he could not see. After he had cleared a strip with the bone, his hand patted the hide, to know that it was clean, and without looking or measuring, he knew how far he should pull it, and started in again, singing to himself as he worked. The dogs circled, waiting for a scrap, but when the boy threw the fat in the bucket he did not miss, so they wandered away.

Her Nistenha and the two aunts carried the deer hide near the stream and put it in a barrel filled with water and ash. Then after many days she and the boy carried the barrel to the stream. He felt his way along the rocks on the bank, and the girl walked beside him, taking his wrist, and together they dumped the barrel into the water. The boy weighted the hide down with a stone to keep it in place and they let the clear water circle it for many days, in the eddy made by the bend in the stream.

After this, when she saw the boy going out along the path she ran to him, and clasped his wrist, and led him along. Perhaps she held too tightly, for he pulled his wrist away and spoke crossly to her, *jaghte oghte*, and other words, which she did not understand, but meant perhaps that he was nearly as old as she, and could make his way himself. She did not mind these cross words, because they were familiar, though she did not speak his tongue. Then she would take her hand away and shove him, and he would shove her lightly back, and she followed behind until she could take his wrist again, more gently.

*From What was Exchanged between his Excellency Joseph
Dudley Esqr. Capn. Gen & Gov in Chief of her Majesties
Province of the Massachusetts Bay &c and The High
and Mighty Seigneur Phillippe de Rigaud, Marquis de
Vaudreuil, Chevalier de l'Ordre Militaire de St. Louis
and Governor General of New France*

Sir,

You will return our prisoners, you tell me, if your Indians are
<u>willing</u> to give them up. This is most choquing. Would you let
a Barbarian determine the fate of a Christian soul? Our tender
English sons and daughters are more crewelly besotted by the
day, and their parents, yt they have been separated from, are most
exercised on acct of them. I trust that you will examine your own
God-given conscience, and after doing so, reconsider yr position.

In this I am
Yr vry humb Srvt
Joseph Dudley Esqr.

Constance

WHEN THEY CAME back for the deer hide, minnows darted around it, and pink crayfish hid underneath. The boy lifted it out of the water, and turned and squeezed the water from it, and put it over his shoulders. Then taking the boy's wrist and holding fast, the girl guided him up the bank. Together they carried the hide to the beam outside the bark house, and scraped it again with the scraping bone.

There was no longer any fat on the hide. They scraped now to remove the hair. Yet when it was her turn to scrape, the girl thought of the scraping differently, which was most strange. The first time, she had thought of the scraping-bone as an English thing, and the scraping had reminded her of something she had done with the English thing, but why she had done such a thing in the English place, she no longer knew, only that her hands seemed to remember how to press the scraping bone, as if they had done it before. So these English words fell away while the way to press the bone remained.

Over many days they came back to the skin and rubbed the brain into it, until the fat softened it. Also by rubbing the brain of the deer, her own skin, which had been very red and rough, became smooth again, so that at night she ran one hand over the other to feel its softness. When Nistenha saw her doing this, she came to her bench to punish her, for children were beaten for these things (such as resting their fingers on the upper lip to feel its softness).

Instead, Nistenha bent down, and ran her own hand over the girl's, and spoke in their tongue. With the other hand she held out the silver spoon, (though it was very late at night) and spooned the corn mush into the girl's mouth as if she were a baby. This was most delightful. There had been English words for the eating times, but here the people ate whenever they would.

Sarah (verso of the loose leaf)

Dear Constance,

I SHOULD willingly endure the trials we suffered again, if I could come to you myself. However be assured, Father will come to redeem you. Though the Lord must intervene most mercifully, for Father has been much abstracted and his hands tremble so that he can not work as he would like. He does not always rightly recall our trials and absence, and whenever the weather is not quite according to the season, cannot tell the month. Or if I remind him of a verse he knew by heart formerly and has forgot he assures me that all is well as he has kept his Commonplace Book for these many years, even before having read Mr. Locke, who calls such a book "the keeper of the Self in the form of memory," which subject is difficult for me to explain to one so young, in as much as I myself do not understand it. Memory being such a variable thing.

Mr. Locke's new method of organization for such a book will not allow Father to forget anything now, he tells me. To that end he works many hours on the new *indices* and I find he is mostly in his study when I want him for anything.

It is a strange little book, but the animals upon which he dilates therein, and certain verses he has selected, are diverting. There are simples and remedies for as many ailments as God has created, some for the sting of serpents found only in the deserts of Sinai.

The Commonplace Book of John Baker

FISHES

Per DAVID PEARSON of *Logblands* in Scotland, Gentleman, *Varieties or, a Svrveigh of Rare and Excellent Matters, Necessary and Delectable for all sorts of persons. Wherein the principal Heads of diverse Sciences are illustrated, rare secrets of Naturall things unfoulded, &c.*

IF THEY CAN be said to breath, seeing they lack pulmons. . . . This question hath been agitated many Ages agoe, both *pro & contra*, as we say; Aristotle . . . denying that they can breath: Plato and divers others of his sect affirming to contrary. For answer to both extremes I could allow for fishes a kind of respiration called refrigeration, since nothing properly can be said to breath but that which hath the instruments of breathing.

Quest. But is it truth of which wee heare of our Navigators, that in the Southerne Seas that they have seene flying fishes, and herring like a foggie or moist cloud fleeing above their heads, and falling againe into the seas with a rushing and flushing?

Answ. Yea I think it possible; for the great creator hath imbued the Aire (as the more noble element of the three) with that perogative; that in it, either fowles or watery creatures might be engendered.

Constance

ALL THROUGH the time of doing things, each morning and evening they went to the little wooden church where the Pear spoke. She understood their tongue a little, and some of the words in Latin.

Yet she remembered the English catechism still, one part after the other, like black frog eggs, floating in their line of clear jelly. Also her mother's words, *Do not speak Latin*, and this she obeyed, and let the sounds run over her like the river, for she knew that her Mother or Father would come for her still, but she no longer asked the Pear when it would be.

Sarah

WOULD THAT women could go freely, as men do! Then I should go to you myself. Instead I endeavor to find a companion for Father; with the Lord such things are made possible. My daughter please *hold on*, do not succumb, deliverance is on the way.

The Commonplace Book of John Baker

SCIENCE

I MOVE TO you O Sciences, for what I seek is certainty! An answer! A sign! Though my interest here is indeed His purpose (as He is before all things and by Him all things consist, Colossians 1:17), yet even within my little library, these good learned men disagree. Is this in fact the sign He sends me?

SUN SPOTS

Per GALILEO GALILEI, *History and Demonstration Concerning Sunspots and Their Phenomena*
If in church some day Your Excellency sees the light of the sun falling upon the pavement at a distance from some broken window pane, you may catch this light upon a flat white sheet of paper, and there will you perceive the *spots*. I might add that nature has been so kind, that for our instruction she has sometimes marked the sun with a spot so large and dark as to be seen merely by the naked eye, though the false and inveterate idea that the heavenly bodies are devoid of all mutation or alteration has made people believe that such a spot was the planet Mercury coming between us and the sun, to the disgrace of past astronomers.

From the *Journal Intime*
of Father Simon René Floquart

THE LORD WORKS in mysterious and wonderful ways! During the lesson in catechism today the English young girl was looking away and willing herself to think on other things, as is her habit, when suddenly He aroused a furious gale, accompanied by thunder and lightning! At this she shrieked and threw her small arms around my girth and buried her head in my stomach, trembling and shaking there.

Now in a soft voice I told the girl that these were no reports of guns but only the work of God who watched over us, and she calmed herself entirely. I felt much as I had in my youth when a feral cat suddenly padded its way onto my chest as I was nodding off. It had slunk inside the door of the chamber I shared with my cousins, without my aunt's knowing. There was that same delicate fear of disturbing the wild one in any way and ending the tender feeling that flooded me, so that I could barely breathe.

Was this not perhaps such a feeling as the Lord might have for those newly drawn to Him, after long resistance? It must be true that He loves each one of these as a prodigal son. What is it in men, asked St. Augustine, that makes them rejoice more for the salvation of a soul that was despaired of than if the peril had been less? But the glorious end has not yet come.

She remained this way with an ear to my belly, I suppose as it is commodious and soft as a pillow; and too, I am aware that it makes a rather immodest amount of noise (at least, on this particular day it did), and upon hearing the growlings there her eyes opened thoughtfully. Then, sighing, she rested her head again.

How can I instruct such a wayward one, a stubborn one, who believes so simply in the falsehoods of her upbringing, and of her parents, obscured in darkness and schisms? And why, Lord Jesus, is my task so difficult, when the other children came to you so easily? Perhaps you wish me to be so weary of my task that I must, as John, recline against you and rest my head upon your shoulder.

As later I sat praying the rosary and simultaneously worrying the question of this lost lamb, the Lord gave me to remember myself as a small boy with a sore heart, months after my mother's departure. I too resisted Him then! One day in a fury I marched to the cathedral, seeking vengeance on Him who had taken her, and moved through the stations of the cross with my little hands in fists, muttering. Yet as I stopped in front of one of the large colorful windows, shaped as a *Catherine Wheel*, my anger stilled suddenly; I marveled there at the intricacies of those radiating petals, their blue and purple effulgence; and overwhelmed by this beauty, I shut my eyes. How amazed was I to find this same window on the back of my eyelids, fully formed, as if it somehow emanated from within me!

And I relate an ordinary experience; every man who walks the earth has had such a glimmer. We respond to beauty, and feel it within in the body. This must be due to the "interior castle," as it was called by our sister, Teresa of Ávila. The soul is housed within us, yet we stand upon the earth in dull complaisance, as if we were as ordinary as stones. Only imagine how magnificent, how beautiful—being the house of the indwelling God Himself—this interior castle must be! And from that day, I have longed to know this light again and abide in it fully.

The English girl will feel such a light within, perhaps in response to the new monstrance, when it arrives, or some other ornament. It is not for you (said the Lord) to arrange it. These are my mysteries; yet know that I will work through her heart, as I worked through yours to find you.

Yes, my Lord, I understand and will be patient. I am filled with affectionate awe, and with such tenderness—when I picture the little girl running to me for safety—that it frightens me. What if my feeling for the girl is that of a parent, rather than a spiritual advisor? I know immediately that this question must be put to my own spiritual director, when next I am in Montréal, and the possibility that he will suggest that Father de Jouy take over her catechism is quite unpleasant to me.

From What was Exchanged between his Excellency Joseph
Dudley Esqr. Capn. Gen & Gov in Chief of her Majesties
Province of the Massachusetts Bay &c and The High
and Mighty Seigneur Phillippe de Rigaud, Marquis de
Vaudreuil, Chevalier de l'Ordre Militaire de St. Louis
and Governor General of New France

Sir,

I am most unwilling to pay ransom for even one of our English
prisoners, as you must know. Can you truly believe that it is *just*
for a Christian to be made a *slave*, possessed by Heathens? In requesting this sum I wonder yt you are not unquiet, as to the state
of your own soul.

Yr Vry Hmbl Svnt,
Joseph Dudley Esqr.

The Commonplace Book of John Baker

Lightening

WHY WE SEE the *lightening* before we hear the noyse.

Per DAVID PEARSON of *Logblands* in Scotland, Gentleman, *Varieties Or, A Svrveigh Of Rare And Excellent matters, necessary and delectable for all sorts of persons. Wherein the principal Heads of diverse Sciences are illustrated, rare secrets of Naturall things unfoulded, &c.*

Now if it be asked; What is the cause, why we see sooner the *lightening* than we hear the thunder clap? That is because our sight both is nobler, and the eye is sooner perceptive of its object, then our eare; as being the more active part and priore to our hearing: beside the visible species are more subtile, and less corporeal then the audible species, this being reall, the former intentionall, as the skillful in Optiks know, and this is the reason why likewise we see the flash ere we heare the noyse of discharged gunnes.

Constance

THEY CALLED HER *Skentsiese*, whose hands were quick for catching fish. So when the moon shone brightly through the firehole, Nistenha took her to the river. Together they put the boat in the water.

The girl held the torch and its light sparkled on the great river. Nistenha climbed out to the rock and lay on the log, draping her hand in the water. Then she shifted and her hand came up, clutching a fish. And the fish flew from her hand to the boat. She clutched another and another as she lay upon the water, until the middle of the boat was shining and flapping.

Upstream, little waves were singing. Downstream, by the rocks, a low drumming. And the owl called with his questioning voice.

But "questioning" was not right, for they said *nan* to ask, and the voice did not go up.

Then Nistenha took the torch, and the girl lay on the rock, and her braids hung in the water. She dangled her arm into the water by the rock, as Nistenha had done. When the fish swam by, her hand knew how to stay, even when the scales brushed it. Then it knew just when to flip, and it came up, holding the fish. So she did this many times, just as Nistenha had done.

In the morning they cleaned the fish, and the girl was amazed, for the same hand that had known how to catch the fish, now knew where to run the knife, as if she had done it many times before. This was very strange.

Perhaps she had dreamed the night-fishing, for it was beautiful when Nistenha lay on the sparkling water, as on a bed of stars.

But when they hung them, the fish were real, and the bark house smelled of fish.

In the chapel the next morning the girl shut her eyes and let the Latin songs wash over her as the shining water in a river, thinking that, as they too were beautiful, and soft, God had surely made them for his own delight. In the same way he must also delight in her whom he had created, out of His mere good pleasure.

So too it was out of his mere good pleasure that he had created them in the bark houses, Nistenha, the aunts and the grandmother, and Philippe Aukwehtá, and Catherine and Mariâ, and Akohsà:tus who had carried her to this place on his shoulders. And he had made all creatures here, the muskrat and the goose and the turtle, whose back was the island of the earth.

Perhaps even Pear he had made. For the Pear did not know he was wicked in speaking Latin.

In the English time it had been a troubling thing, whether she would sit by the Lord's right hand forevermore, but now she perceived that he would miss her very much if he could not have her by him forevermore, for all along he had kept her close to him.

From the *Journal Intime*
of Father Simon René Floquart

THIS MORNING THE savage mother and her adopted English daughter came to Mass with their hair fashioned in a most extraordinary manner, each in two plaits, though the married women normally wear theirs in one that runs down the back. The adoptive mother, her hair having been cut to the scalp during her mourning, still has very short hair, so that her own plaits stuck straight out from her head. It seemed to me that the girl had braided her own hair and her mother's as well, for both were decorated with a strange mess of feathers and French buttons and dyed porcupine quills of red and blue, but also pine needles—which, because of the pitch, the savages never use in hair or headdress. As the savages never reprimand their children, I suppose the mother had given the girl license to create what was more suitable for the carnival than for Mass in a wilderness station.

In Mass I could not help but regard these two with some fascination, during which the girl, squeezing her eyes shut as usual, opened *one* eye most cautiously, as if to gauge my reaction, whether I admired their colorful headdresses, or no, at which I could not help but smile at their ludicrous appearance (for with this colorful mess on her head, the one eye squeezed shut, the girl resembled a tropical bird). Catching me at this, she rather fiercely closed both eyes again, and even turned her head from me, her shoulders shaking with that which I soon realized was not anger but stifled laughter. At this I struggled not to laugh myself, which is difficult once one has entertained the possibility.

What lightness came to my heart then! On any normal day their voices raised together as they sing the psalms fills my heart with awe, and this day especially, I felt humbled and grateful for what God has wrought here, awed that I have been allowed to follow in the steps of my dear mother, and to be part of the Lord's work in our humble mission! No matter that the girl does not yet join them in the song. I feel that it will not be long before we will have won her soul for the Lord.

Sarah

14 September 1704

Dear Peter,

THE LORD BE praised, for He works in wonderful and mysterious ways to ensure our deliverance and redemption. Mr. Baker
has word from Reverend Cartwright that you have been ransomed and redeemed and safely returned to the fold after nearly
one year of living wildly as an Indian. (We heard these tales with
some alarm for it was said that you had the painted countenance
of a barbarian, and that you singlehandedly killed a *moose* with
bow and arrow, and butchered it withal!) I pray that upon your
return, God has made you to appear again as a reverent English
boy, which ever you were.

What great praise we give the Lord for your timely
deliverance.

*In a little wrath I hid my face from thee for a moment; but with ev-
erlasting kindness will I have mercy on thee, saith the Lord thy Redeemer.*

As for my daughter Constance, we were parted at the end
of the journey after you were led away; she was also taken by
an *Indian* to Canada. Mr. Baker my husband will go hither to
redeem her, and if it pleases the Lord, with a young guide such
as yourself, who knows the way better than he, who is inured to
such travel, the journey may prove profitable. We are gathering
such funds as could compensate your father for your absence.

Please write, if God has made you willing to entertain our
proposition. Mr. Baker has written your father requesting the
same; only with this letter I appeal to your young goodness, as

you have some knowledge of the persons involved, and their sore hearts withal.

In the name of God Most Merciful,
Sarah Baker

From the *Journal Intime*
of Father Simon René Floquart

THE SUMMER HAS ended, the nights grow cold, and the savages' preparation for winter reminds me that I requested the new monstrance in spring and have had no word that we will receive one. Today I found myself in tears of frustration, which I examined carefully to determine why the silence of the Superior in this matter is so disturbing to me. I can explain the presence of Christ in the Sacrament with my words, as Father Dublon has done before me; and young Father de Jouy, of course, is able to do so if anything I say is unclear to them. However, the *presence of Christ in the Sacrament* can be explained in words. Not so the *beauty* that conveys His mystery!

Considered this way, is any beauty *mere* ornament? The *Maestà* of Duccio came to mind. As the whole painting is glutted with gold, as even the *sky above* is gold, is it not in this way inherently numinous? With chagrin I recalled my earlier attempts to draw those same scenes of the passion for the savages. My drawings were *of interest* to the people. But what we seek is a response from the soul, and nothing less than amazement.

Still, we find a *golden sky* in many works which fall short of the *Maestà*. Our soul is ignited in that particular work by the men and women and angels of the artist's imagination, whose eyes catch those of the onlooker, so that one feels one is seen by them. Even the child Christ himself is solemn and knowing, and seems to look at one directly, out of time, aware of all that will befall Him, the sins of the one who stands staring at Him (of what would these eyes accuse me today? Crying over the monstrance, perhaps?) and His own adorable sacrifice.

So, brooding upon all of this, wondering how in a wilderness station one might possibly explain the *interior castle*, wondering whether the monstrance was perhaps being fashioned expressly for us and this was the reason for the delay, and that, when it arrived, it would be more ornate than I had even imagined, I found myself walking up behind the palisade to the maple grove on the hill, drawn there by the leaves turning their colors, but not truly seeing them (for I was worrying about the monstrance, and the role of ornament, as I have said, as if I were in argument with the superior), and I made my way to a deer path through the grove, a narrow corridor of yellow maples. As I was drawn into this corridor, suddenly a wind came up, and with a loud rush, bright golden leaves filled the air, swirling around me, and carpeting the path in front of me the same bright gold.

Now do you see? asked the Lord. For I have not only inspired the artist, I am the artist at work. In the words of St. Ignatius, They should often be exhorted to seek God our Lord *in all things*. . . . In this way those of our order might become contemplatives even in action.

As I made my way home I looked down on our little mission, on the savages walking their paths below me, and on the tops of the longhouses, where beans and corn were laid out in thanks to the sun, the sight of which had agitated me in the past. But now, I heard the tender voice of the Lord in my breast. "It is I who works through them, even as I work through you, and I love them as I love you." Oh, to know and understand them fully! To speak the savage tongue from the heart! If only He would bestow this understanding on me suddenly, as my mother suddenly could translate the gospel into the Huron—"It flowed as a gift!"

Constance / Skentsiese

THEIR TONGUE CAME flooding in, as if she remembered it. She understood when they spoke to each other in the bark house. And no longer were their words heavy on her tongue, so that she might answer them, or say to them what she liked. Neither were there times here for speaking or not speaking, nor must she ask permission or cleave herself in two and become the quiet one.

She watched herself for a time (as if outside of herself, as she had watched her hand remember to catch the fish) and it was very like watching another, for what she wanted to say came quickly, so that it was not Constance speaking but the one they called Skentsiese.

Ha' o ki wà hi, come on then, she said to Philippe, and he growled at her, but he came, and Catherine and Mariâ came. She showed them that by taking their elbows they might make a chair for Philippe and lift him up (he pouted and squirmed, but once up, his chin lifted like a king's, for he sat high above them) The game was called Honeypot, she told them, an English word.

They repeated it, *hanipa*.

Qu'est ce que ça veut dire?

She could not remember, if it meant another thing. She remembered only the name for this game.

From . . . *the terable captivitie and wonderfull redemption*
of Sarah Baker

MANY WEEKS PASSED. It grew cold, and we waited for the clement weather. My husband had improved, yet, I thought, he was not altogether sound of mind. I thought of my daughter's small voice yet saw her a little unclearly now as in a dream, and I woke to think of my childless state, and was downcast. Then came the time of weaning, and the poor cows bawling to their calves across the fence that parted them, which rent my heart, though I well knew that it was only their bags which galled the cows, and when their milk dried, they would stop. Still they stood at their fences, bawling, one to the other, all the night long, and into the day. Two nights I did not sleep for the terrible noise, but the morning after the second night, they were quiet.

Still they stood at their fences, looking. But they did not remember what they looked for.

From the *Journal Intime*
of Father Simon René Floquart

IN THIS TIME of year I often wake in glad expectation. Sometimes this is roused by the sight of fresh snow—a rolling, white sea against which our tall pines stand so majestically dark and green—but there is also the expectation of the Nativity, and the memory of former times, when a letter from my mother would arrive for me each year late in Advent. Sometimes to know that the loved one has thought of us is enough to sustain us, and throughout the year I invented many sentiments and longings on my mother's behalf. Yet the simple sight of her handwriting, confirming her concern for my soul, was enough to fill my eyes with tears, and I praised God for the means to commune with her that was outside of time, as the Lord Himself is outside of time, and so most wonderful, miraculous.

Indeed, our savages do take the acts of writing and reading to be no smaller miracle than that of the loaves and the fishes! Shortly after my arrival, Father Dublon wrote them two notes, read each one aloud, and asked the savages to deliver them to me: Père Floquart, the first note read, "put on your hat." When I put the hat upon my head, how they gasped! Then I passed my eyes over the second note ("take off your hat") and took off the hat, and they laughed heartily, asking, as a child does, *encore!* What lightness in my heart! I was able to laugh with them and envisioned many such moments to come. Shortly thereafter my hat went missing, and I wrote the first of many letters to the Superior, requesting its replacement. Yes, perhaps I never report on our mission without also requesting that something be sent us. The requests are all for necessities, however. I do consider a monstrance a necessity. But I will not dwell upon that now, for my soul is heartened by what has passed today.

Just after the Mass I asked them if they would like to practice the songs for the upcoming Nativity, and they sang the *Puer Natus* perfectly. They had forgotten nothing. This moved me strongly, as I had only heard them singing it together with Father Dublon. Without his somber bass tones, without Father de Jouy (who is often so enthused that he is carried away, and drowns out all around him) and without their men, who are hunting, the women and girls sing most beautifully in the Latin tongue, for they exaggerate and extend each o very roundly, allle *looo* ia, Jer *ooo* salem. With their lips pursed and their brows knit in earnestness, their expressions sincere and sweet, they embody perfectly the spirit of the faith. It stirred me to tears, as if the song were in the second mode.

Then the Lord interposed most delightfully, and I detected a new element to their chorus. The English girl had begun to sing with them, forgetting her rule of silence. How earnestly she sings! The insistent, clear voice of a child that is nearly a shout, and in its guileless fullness makes us smile. Also in the way of children, she was not impeded by the words she did not know, instead sailing along on the vowels, a bit behind the others, and casting a glance at her mother, who watched her most proudly, and at one moment, placed a tender hand upon her head.

The Commonplace Book of John Baker

CURES AND SIMPLES ctd.

(Per HEINRICH CORNELIUS, Agrippa's *De Occulta Philoso-phia libri tres*)

PLINY REPORTS that there are red toads that make their home in briars, and are full of sorcery and do wonderful things. For the small bone that is in its left side, when cast into cold water, makes it immediately become hot. It restrains the attacks of dogs. Added to a drink, it arouses love and quarrels. When tied to someone, it arouses lust. On the other hand, the little bone that is in the right side cools hot water, and it will not become hot again unless the bone is taken out. It cures quartan fevers, when tied in a fresh lamb's skin, and prevents other fevers and love and lust. And the spleen and heart of these toads make an effective remedy against the poisons that are drawn from those animals.

From the *Journal Intime*
of Father Simon René Floquart

OUR NEW MONSTRANCE was delivered today. I might describe it as an *ordinary* monstrance in the southern style, a simple cross atop a sun bursting forth in filigree. In short, it is rather plain. There are no gems embedded, or images fashioned in the base. Nevertheless, the lunette is clear and the gold plate so bright that the savages were quite transfixed by it, the rays of this sun drawing their eyes toward the Host, where they rested, dwelling upon the Most Holy Body of Christ without remembering that this was what they did.

Only my young charge (for whom I have suggested Marie-Ange as a Christian name), quickly looked away, as I have seen her cast her eyes down from the cross at the back of the chapel. The savages are easier to instruct in such matters. It is much more difficult to explain such a thing to one who has been previously indoctrinated with falsehoods.

During the girl's spiritual direction this afternoon, I recalled a painting of young Juliana of Liège, which I had seen in Padua. In this painting, the girl's hands softly hold the monstrance and her eyes are *downcast*, and gaze upon it most tenderly. I told the girl that Juliana was orphaned at five years of age, and that she had been scarcely older than Marie-Ange herself when she went to the leper colony and had her vision of the moon with its dark spot. What was the dark spot, she wondered. *Oui!* A good question. It was the missing holy day, I told her, that we now call Corpus Christi. *Pour quoi?* As it commemorates the Body of Christ in the Sacrament.

At this she looked at me with interest, and thus encouraged, I attempted to sketch the sweet face of Juliana that I remembered from the painting. It wasn't until I displayed my effort that I noticed that in trying to fashion the soft dent of Juliana's philtrum, I had instead drawn something like a set of pincers emerging from the nostrils; and the bowed mouth was much too big, rendering the image ridiculous rather than tender. Still it is strange that I felt very sorry for my poor Juliana, before recalling that I should be sorry for myself!

Sometimes I imagine God looking at my own form as tenderly as I looked at Juliana's on my paper. (Oh dear, I imagine Him saying, that is not quite what I meant to do. But this man has, after all, a sincere longing for Me.) Of course, the Potter has fashioned His clay for His own purpose; it is merely diverting to imagine Him speaking so regretfully. Yet there is something true in that *tenderness*, I believe. I have felt it in quiet moments of contemplation.

From ... *the terable captivitie and wonderfull redemption of Sarah Baker*

THE LORD HELPED me to bear my waiting but many things reminded me daily, such as the attic where still was kept that cradle, which was Ezariah's cradle and of course it was Hannah's long before that and also Constance and John's (and also baby Charles, baby Elizabeth who only rested there a day before they went to be with God), now *all but Constance* gone to be with God. Or my loom would remind me, for I knew that as soon her feet reached the treadles she would work with her hands, willingly.

And I pleaded with the Lord, O help me, for I am downcast. O, I will not let thee go, except thou bless me.

Constance / Skentsiese

IN A DREAM she saw the others clearly. Hold fast to *John*, Mother told her, but she could not hold fast. She disobeyed and *John* was not. O *Ezariah*, Mother said, *Ezariah* my babe and he was not and *General* was not. *Par terre. John* was not.

From the *Journal Intime*
of Father Simon René Floquart

SHE CAME TO me quite unexpectedly and said that she would like to confess as the others did. I dared not show my delight at this turn of events. Had the beauty of the monstrance done its glorious work after all? But these things are between the girl and God. Perhaps, seeing her savage mother and grandmother and aunts come and go from the chapel, leaving it lighthearted as one feels when one has done one's penance, she desired to know it for herself. I explained that she would have to make the sign of the cross, to repeat after me the act of contrition (as she had denied Our Lady, and refused to learn it) and she merely nodded, as if she had never crossed her arms or shut her eyes or resisted at all.

The sign of the cross she made as if she had done it many times before, but when I asked for her confession she began in English (too quickly spoken for me to understand), turning to French when she recalled my presence, and falling from those into the savage tongue, which now prevails with her over the other two.

When I pronounced the absolution I felt its beauty strongly, and found myself in tears of compassionate awe. If she did not understand these words (as I had not understood hers), still the Holy Spirit had moved through them. Her shaking stopped, and though her eye was vacant, she no longer seemed distraught, and repeated the formal act of contrition and her penance as I guided her, in a voice devoid of emotion, so that I wondered if she even knew that she spoke.

Constance / Skentsiese

EZARIAH, *elle a dit*, O, Ezariah my babe.
He was Ezariah, he was not Ezariah. He was not.
Constance, hold fast to John, but he eloped, down the stairs,

Non
Thó nonkwá ionsásewe' (That   way   gobackthere)
the eye that mocketh his father
let the ravens of the valley pluck it out

all of them down the dark stairs

Sarah

My Constance,

If I could send these words, you would know that Father is on the way to reclaim you, with the young guide by his side. Your redemption is coming! God has sent me a sign. Today as I was washing my cheese, a yellow gib-cat appeared on the steps. I fed him a pinch.

Document of Baptism

On Tuesday 10 April 1705 was baptized by me the priest under-signed the little English Constance Baker born at Hartfield Hills on the 19th of August 1696 in New England of the marriage of John Baker and Sarah (Brown) Baker. She has *previously abjured the Calvinistic heresy* and having been taken at Hartfield Hills in New England the 11 March 1704 and brought to Canada, is living at St. Ignace Mission at La Rivière des Anges. Her English name of *Constance* has been changed to *Marie-Ange*.

Floquart Priest

The Commonplace Book of John Baker

Tomorrow I set forth for Canada, there to redeem my daughter Constance. If it pleases the Lord, I shall soon relate the story of my journey, and her blessed redemption withal.

From the *Journal Intime*
of Father Simon René Floquart

ALL IS ORCHESTRATED by our benevolent God, who
knows our hearts, and wishes most ardently for our salvation in
Him! I am bathed in extraordinary delight today, but why do I
feel this more strongly than on many other days when a savage
or Englishman has been baptized? I doubted myself, doubted
the Lord's promise, even; at times it seemed the next trader
who passed through this wilderness station might easily spirit
her away; she was, I know, eager for that. However, she, having suffered heresies, then being ripped most terribly from all
that was known to her, was thus opened to His mysterious ways
which have prevailed with her most wonderfully, and my heart is
filled with a warmth, lightness and joy, a confirmation of my path
and duty. For He gives us these trials so that in the midst of the
dark night we should have only Him to rest upon (though even
His presence may, as part of the trial, hide itself for a time), then
finally He draws us closer, and only then apportions our reward.

*From What was Exchanged between his Excellency Joseph
Dudley Esqr. Capn. Gen & Gov in Chief of her Majesties
Province of the Massachusetts Bay &c and The High
and Mighty Seigneur Phillippe de Rigaud, Marquis de
Vaudreuil, Chevalier de l'Ordre Militaire de St. Louis
and Governor General of New France*

14 April 1705

Sir,

AS YOU MUST understand, it is only in my *power* to send your
prisoners who are in the hands of the French. The savages are not
my subjects, but my allies. I have attempted to make this clear,
yet you persist in misunderstanding the nature of our relation.
Nevertheless, in order to appease you, I have consulted the King
my master, who has ordered the Superior that each prisoner
should be allowed to choose for himself, whether to return, or
not. You mention that many prisoners are children. The Superior
assures me that these savages are much concerned with *the will* of
a child, often granting him the puissance of a grown man. As to
what the children will answer, I can not promise anything where
that is concerned!

Whatever your objections may be to this offer, you must
admit that it is more generous than yours to me in the matter of
our French prisoners.

Your most humble servant,
Seigneur Phillipe de Rigaud, Marquis de Vaudreuil

From the *Journal Intime*
of Father Simon René Floquart

BECAUSE HE FOLLOWS light with darkness so that we cling
to Him....

Today we received two pieces of news from our courier. The
first is that the English father of Marie-Ange can be expected
within the week. Nearly as disturbing is that Governor Vaudreuil
has promised the English Dudley at Boston that we will permit
any of the captive English children to return *who wish to*, even if it
is against the will of the savages who own them. Considering that
"there is no authority except that which God has established," in
the words of St. Ignatius our founder, we have no choice in the
matter. Because her savage mother is not allowed to be present,
there is a danger that the sight of her English father, or some
heretical words of his, will convince Marie-Ange to return with
him.

I did suggest to the savage mother that perhaps she and
Marie-Ange might wish to go to the woods for a week, on some
pretext that I might truthfully explain to the superior, but she
looked at me curiously, so that I wondered if she did not understand my words. Then she said, *d'accord*, which I took to mean
that they would indeed go to the woods. Instead she added that
she would send Marie-Ange to her English father when the time
came, as lightly as if she were telling me that she would "send
her" to learn her catechism.

I remain hopeful, however, that this tender seed we have
planted here will prove hard to uproot. I do sense an affection
between Marie-Ange and her savage mother. Savage women do
not, as a rule, caress their children, but the two walk back and

forth daily to the fields together by way of the chapel, and when the several longhouses left together for the fishing trip Marie-Ange was not left behind this time, which I only discovered when she did not appear in Mass and the grandmother told me, as I understood her, "Two do not part."

I see her working together with them, to cut the earth before the planting, shoulder to shoulder with the two aunts of the longhouse and the toddling boy, or carrying him on her hip. We have learned from previous Relations that their daily work forms part of the custom of requickening; it is the tasks they willingly perform that weave the children into the fabric of life here, and from these same tasks they derive their names and function within the family.

Still I am anxious and sleep eludes me. I have prayed to God to send me a sign, whether she will desire to go back with her father, or no, and I hope that today He has done so. For I saw her with the odd band of three, Mariä and Catherine, and blind Philippe, spinning together until they grew dizzy, and fell down. I have seen them spinning thus before, and found it only foolishness, and a child's game. But today I recalled that St. Francis commanded Brother Masseo to spin in the crossroad to determine whether God would have them go to Siena, Florence or Arezzo, so Brother Masseo twirled and grew dizzy and fell in the direction of Siena.

Then too, young Teresa of Ávila spun with her siblings, chanting *forever and forever.*

As I write this I am plagued by doubt (as Brother Masseo murmured in the crossroads, for spinning there seemed to him mere child's play!)

Remember! St. Francis restored peace to that walled city of Siena, and there led many souls to salvation!

Constance / Skentsiese / Marie-Ange

Father.

His body stiff like a fishing spear. His chin with long hairs like a bear.

    ___ ! (Con-stans.)

She squatted herself as they did to talk (but Pear did not squat himself, he did not like to muddy his dress).

His eyes were too light, like the eyes of a wolf.

Speak to him, *repond, dit-le quelque chose*, Marie-Ange, Pear said.

Father put it. *Read.*

Which is the fifth Commandment. Say.

her mouth cudent say, *mais* the book ran as the river, running and blurring, as when tears

The fifthcommandment forbiddethneglecting ordoing any thingagainst the Honourand Duty . . . in their Several Places&Relations. . . .

Thó nonkwá ionsásewe' (That way gobackthere)

Cleave thyself in two

mais

jaghte oghte she said (maybe not)

From the *Journal Intime*
of Father Simon René Floquart

BLESSED BE GREAT Jesus, whose gracious providences are always adorable!

The girl's English father arrived today from Boston, with a young boy in tow. I took him to be the brother of our Marie-Ange, but remembered that her brothers had "perished." In fact, the young man was only an English boy, who had marched northward with the father. He was perhaps a servant, yet his manner docile and polite. He spoke a little French, then English for the two of them, addressing me in the father's place. The father seemed unwilling to look at me.

Père de Jouy ran to fetch Marie-Ange from where she was planting with her mother; she arrived with dirt covering her hands and under her fingernails, her hair greased with the pungent eel fat, her skin also shining with the same, and wearing her leather tunic and leggings.

The father started when he saw her. This I might have predicted, but strangely he did not *then* move to embrace her, but kept apart from her, scowling, speaking a few harsh words. She squatted in front of him most miserably, fixing her eyes on the ground, and halted as she spoke in English, turning to Père de Jouy to mutter easily in the savage tongue. (Indeed, a child still young, who has begun to exchange one mother for another, must also exchange her mother tongue, so that it is the savage one that now comes more easily, and from the heart.)

I studied the father's face in order to glean the subject of his remarks, when suddenly he looked familiar to me, as if I had known him all of my life! Indeed, with his grey beard and short fringe, he bore a resemblance to Joseph in the painting of the Holy Family in Avignon. Both father and mother are stern there, scowling at young Jesus, but their anger barely hides their fear, and each holds an open palm, asking *Where have you been?* A question that loving parents everywhere ask their children! In fact our Lord Jesus had come from His dispute at the Temple with the Pharisees—yes even, imagines the artist, at that tender age, for in his rendering, our Savior is still a child—and what moves us is this ordinary parental love, which is concomitant with fear.

Of course, this English father's scowling only served to frighten the child. He held a book out in front of her, perhaps an English catechism, and implored her to read from it.

She recoiled. Yet his hand, holding the book, trembled mightily! Yes, one of my age could not fail to understand him, for his worn body spoke for him, saying that he had ridden and marched these many long days and slept upon the hard ground; and his clothes also spoke, as they were dirty and ragged; and his brow, deeply lined with care: all offices of love.

Who truly knows a man such as this, outside of his maker?

I felt a wave of pity for the Englishman. But I praise God that the girl was not similarly affected!

In this, the Lord's triumph, I was filled with compassionate awe.

Constance / Skentsiese / Marie-Ange

Elle est ou ma mère?
blue dress, pockets. Cut a switch.
O, *elle a dit*, Ezariah my babe.

The Commonplace Book of John Baker

THE LORD BE praised. He vouchsafed my arrival to Canada; ensured that young Peter recalled the way most truly; He made the sun to shine upon us and the wind at our backs in excess of rain and cold and splenetick climes; He designed all discomforts and tryals of our journey so that they should be easily conquered and quickly dispatched; He was pleased to endow the heart of every salvage we encountered by the way with His own Goodwill and peacefulness. Now I have safely returned. Through all difficulties His mercy has preserved me most wonderfully sound in body.

Mr. Schulyer took me to the encampment where our daughter lives. It galls my heart to relay here that she would not parley with me; neither would she regard me in any way, and regarded the ground as she spoke. She has the appearance of a salvage in every way.

I was, in the end, convinced she has forgotten the English tongue, for a few times she attempted words in the French as if to use the only foreign tongue she knows. In former times she was a child who was inclined to prattle on in English about anything, asking questions enough to merit punishment; yet I found her at the time of my visit shy, unwilling, and empty of any way to convey whatever she might think.

The Priest accompanied me along with a young popish apprentice (who wore his red hair long as a devil); she spoke to the young one in the salvage tongue and he relayed her words to me, which were not many. Simply, she "does not think" she will return. I asked him to tell her that she belonged to us, and more importantly, to God's covenant in New England (the Priest

178

translated this as *Boston*, at which I stopped to correct him); but she repeated in their strange Indian tongue that she did not think she would come, which uncertainty made me hopeful, yet the young apprentice Priest told me the prevarication is part of their tongue, and always accompanies even the staunchest refusal.

It was my dearest wish that she return with me.

Still, it is more important that she remember her faith, never to be swayed by these popish fancies with which these *thimblerig-gers* have surely presented her.

When asked to repeat her catechism she could recite a few words directly after my speaking them, but with vacant eye, and that merely to comply with my wishes.

God has made known to us the obligations her pious up-bringing imposes upon her. A child who so stubbornly casts off the advantage of a Christian home is ungrateful in the eyes of God, and is, to Him, worse than a child of a heretic or an Ethiopian.

I pray now that we may devise some other means for her redemption. With the Lord's help she will remember her mother tongue, her faith, her English home, the image of which must rest within her dormant, for this is the way, I have found, of most memory, that things which seem lost to us have only hidden until the time when it is the Lord's pleasure to have us find them.

But if it is not so? If by some measure instead her mind has been erased, as sometimes occurs (below, per *Aristotle*), then another remedy must be sought. We must then consider the use of force, with the help of our Governor.

Surely one cannot steal what is already one's own.

MEMORY ctd.

One must think of the affection, which is produced by means of perception in the soul . . . as being like *a sort of picture*, the having of which we say is memory. For the change that occurs marks in a sort of imprint of the sense-image, as people do who seal things with signet rings. . . .

This is also why *memory does not occur in those who are subject to a lot of movement, because of some trouble or because of their time of life, just as if the change and seal were falling on running water. . . . And this is why the very young and the old have poor memory, since they are in a state of flux, the former because they are growing, the latter because they are wasting away.*

From the *Journal Intime*
of Father Simon René Floquart

TODAY I LEAVE for Montréal for spiritual direction. Père de Jouy led them in their Mass as I made my preparations. I slipped in as he began the invocation, and tears came to my eyes. His voice is lower and seems to have acquired a new gravity.

In my last spiritual direction I did not tell my advisor of my fatherly affection for the girl for fear that he would insist that Père de Jouy take over her spiritual advisement. Now, Lord, I am willing. He will do for the girl. He will do.

My Lord, help me. For as I prepare to leave this place I am filled with foreboding. Is it for my journey, for what the superior will tell me, and the pain of that examination? Or even for the journey itself?

Whenever I leave a place, I remember my mother departing "for a time," never to return.

Could Père de Jouy be allowed to make the journey with me? No. I cannot explain, even to myself, why I feel the need of his companionship.

Trust. All will be well.

John Baker to Deacon Sheldon

10 June 1705

Sir,

I WRITE TO plead the case of my daughter, Constance Baker, nine years of age. Sixteen months have passed since her captivation and it is now a matter of urgency, and of her *Soul*.

Our *Governor Dudley* well knows that the French *Governor Vaudreuil* prevaricates, and falsely insists he is exerting the utmost effort to release the English prisoners, whereas it is clear that he leaves it in the hands of the French papists and the salvages who have no interest in returning them. As these English children have been submitted to all manner of witchcraft and perswasions, *their own will*, as the French governor has written it, is hardly to be determined! I humbly submit to you and to Governor Dudley that the only measure remaining may be an *offer of exchange*, of a personage valuable to New France in some capacity, such as one *among their priests*, so that the governor is bound to exert his puissance in the matter, as he has heretofore falsely insisted that he does.

I am, sir, in this
Yr Vry Humbl Srvt
John Baker
Hartfield Falls

From *The Confessions* of Father Simon René Floquart, Part Two (Boston)

THERE IS ONLY a little light through the loupe-hole in the cell, so that I know it is morning. Just this small thing—to be able to tell night from day—is a grace. Soon the shadow will descend, so I must make haste, and finish while I still have use of my eyes, which fail more each day in the perpetual darkness.

Last night God saw fit to soften the jailer's heart toward me, so that he finally brought me the ink pen and paper I requested. As He inspired St. John of the Cross to write poems from his little cell, the Lord has given me the words that follow, to complete my confessions. I can see them all at once before me, as God saw the world before its creation. My hand trembles in excitement and my words now *flow as a gift*.

Here in the cell there is barely room for me to sit, a tiny bench of stone and the close walls which graze my arms and legs on each side. At first my mind suffered agitations which caused me to try to shift myself, but the confinement of the cell itself did not permit it, rather I must sit quite straight. (Occasionally I can wriggle myself halfway to a standing position as I do when trying to catch the remaining light through the loupe-hole, but as the cell is not tall enough and I must hunch there, I cannot stay long and it is nearly impossible to write with only the stone wall as a sort of vertical table, against which I must press both tablet and paper).

Sitting here in the cell for the first few hours there was no pain, as my back was supported by the stone wall, yet this absence in fact caused my mind to run wildly. For I had no way to know if I would spend the rest of my days in the cell, if I would be tortured here, or starved to death. But as I did not know the answers to these questions, soon my mind had run through them and I sat alone in the dark, praying to God to do His will, and for my own strength to submit readily to Him in whatever was to come. And yet no comfort came from the prayer, but instead great dread. I felt that I was indeed alone, and that God had forsaken me.

Waves of doubt came over me, and again I endeavored to call to Him, but His response was only silence. Hours went by, and I was truly in a dark night of the soul. Only later I realized that His answer had not been in words.

Instead He sent me bodily pains, which migrated from my back to my ankles where they rubbed at the stone, to a general pain that seemed to come from the knowledge that I could not shift my body, the body itself resenting this inertia internally, so inwardly sending heavy thick pains of a strange nature, shooting from one ankle to the opposite shoulder, or for what felt to me the better half of a day, clasping the head as in a vise squeezing ever more firmly.

Then admonishing myself (for had my fingers been severed from the knuckle, had my own flesh been lopped off, roasted and eaten before my very eyes?) I endeavored to find consolation in those tortures which I was not made to endure. Yet what entered my heart instead was a fierce jealousy of that very adorable suffering that was given to the martyrs of New France, who had been drawn close to Christ in Gethsemane when their sweat turned to blood as His had.

This jealousy made me contrast what I imagined would be my ignoble death with those of our great martyrs, and it took hold so strongly that I doubted Father Regnaut's Relation of the taking of St. Ignace and of Father Brébeuf's death, as Father Regnaut had not witnessed these things, but they were only relayed to him "by Christian savages worthy of belief." Yet, I thought suddenly (and indeed the doubt had lurked previously, in earlier years, and whenever it arose I had merely tamped it down, knowing it to be wicked) the *pouring of boiling water* onto a victim is not mentioned in any other Relations of torture at the hands of the Iroquois. And if this detail were spurious, had Father Brébeuf truly endured his torture while praying gratefully to God, when even Christ our Lord had buried His face in Veronica's soft veil, and asked His Father, "Why hast thou forsaken me?" What then could I really know of the Relations themselves, upon which I had relied for so many years? What if these had been written to glorify the fathers of New France, instead of our Father in Heaven?

This was the first stage. And then, as a wild horse is suddenly exhausted by his bucking and straining at the bridle, I struggled no more. There was my breath, entering and leaving the body quite demurely, whispering along my philtrum as if it had been doing so all along.

Oddly, the great pain was there too, now in my back, where my pelvis was forced, on the stone bench, to tilt forward as the bench did, compressing the spine; and now perhaps after half an hour, moving under my shoulder blade with the sensation of a carving knife. And yet it was as if I stood watching the body in its pain, a dispassionate observer. And following this stage, which may have lasted several hours, a blue light came flickering against the eyelids (much as it had at the Catherine Wheel window) and my palate, along with the jaw, the tongue and all the muscles of speech and language, all melted into a warm suffusion of light, which passed through me, from the mouth where it had generated, to the crown of the head, and then to the toes and back again, running fluidly for I know not how long, for I stopped thinking in any way, and can only say that I was overtaken by the presence of a greater love than I had imagined possible, so that when I came again to my senses, I was moved to tears at the realization of what had passed (for as soon as I *thought of it*, it ended and I longed for its return).

Though I had known before with my mind the precious nature of this animating spirit, I felt the truth of it—that it is goodness without form, uncreated; that it abides in me; that I live by its grace, the tremendous indwelling love of God, which accepts even my inability to abide in it.

Indeed, I wondered then—and I perceived that it had withdrawn a little *in order* for me to wonder—if God's love for us was so great that we must fail, in this life, to abide in it, and to know and comprehend it (if in its pure state it was that goodness without form, uncreated, that still throbbed gently within me), how could we cling to our own apprehension of it? Must we not also make room for others who long for this formless love, who believe and misapprehend (in our eyes) as we must necessarily do? For all of us might be as little blind Philippe—led gently along the path, stumbling, knowing little of where we went. Yet we did not even know that we were blind! If God's love were vast enough to include us in our smallness and misapprehension, did He not necessarily also love those who longed for Him and yet misapprehended Him even more greatly? Were not all of our hearts *restless*, in the words of St. Augustine, until they *rested* in Him? And did it not follow that the death of His only Son was meant to save everyone who longed for Him? So it seemed to me that as man had one language before Babel (from which all deviations had sprung), so we all longed for and called upon the same God, were all one, were enveloped in His formless love; and all paths we trod with longing truly emanated from Him, as various beams go out from the sun; so that when I saw the Pit of Hell it was empty of souls, and when I saw Heaven, it teemed with even those savages who had never heard of Christ, for still they knew Him in the golden and formless light that animated every living being.

Then I began to *think* in the savage tongue just as if it were my mother tongue, and I perceived that the Lord had fashioned this tongue so that the verb played its part in every *thing* which He had created; because He was not done on the seventh day, but *is* ever present, and there is no object or noun in the world that the Lord *is* not also *continually creating*.

In the midst of this vision I was suddenly interrupted by the jailer, who whispered through the loupe-hole that the Governor

Vaudreuil had secured my release in exchange for the English girl Marie-Ange, at the insistence of the English Governor Dudley.

I felt a flooding of affectionate awe and happiness, followed by relief—that things would return to the way they had been, and should be. But this was not only for myself—as I had moved beyond my pain and discomfort and had accepted fully whatever would happen to me—but for the English parents, whose hearts in this warm union of light I felt as my own!

As in a painter's vision, I saw clearly the girl's English father with his grey fringe, still scowling because he must reprove the girl, yet there shone in his eyes the love of David crying, *Oh Absalom, Absalom, my son*! Beside him sat the English mother in a lapis lazuli robe, her white hair falling down her back, her enormous hands cupped, ready to *receive* the child, her dark eyes brimming with tears of joy.

Yes, what I had longed for, the pure and unmatched love that only a mother can to give her child, this English mother had for her daughter—was waiting, longing, to give it! How fitting that I should be the one to bring them into each other's arms! For here on earth, I thought, it is only the love of a mother that can truly secure us and make us complete. If such love is withdrawn, one forever holds oneself stiffly. One cannot truly experience affection of any kind. Had not even Père Dublon cried *Maman* as his last word on this earth? Perhaps it had been no sin. For only *through* our mothers, could we learn to love our neighbors as ourselves.

Do I make myself clear? I did not love these English parents as one should love one's enemy. Instead I saw through the same veil, had the same mote on my eye. I lost sight of the purity of the one true church within this vision and my mind, for a few terrifying moments, became that of a heretic. It was sweet and warm and suffused with light, because that is the way of the devil, who (just as the cuckoo lays her eggs in another's nest) enters where the Holy Spirit has gently and warmly passed, in order to confound us. Let us not forget that Lucifer was the most beautiful angel, and knows to deceive with the ways of angels, who are full of light. All these sympathies and tender feelings the devil did send me, in order to entice me to stay quiet, to let myself be ransomed, and return to my comfort. I have written of my first intimations of danger when I came to love the young English girl as a father might love a daughter, yet before this day I had not truly known how sentiment and worldly love can impede the soul, and lure it into sin.

I saw suddenly that I had longed to be loved by my own mother in the incomprehensible way, the way that only God could love me. Until now, this misapprehension had kept me apart from Him!

And for several minutes or an hour, even as I saw my sin, I was helpless against it, as I was overcome by another image, also clear in my mind's eye as a painting. Against a numinous golden sky, the English girl ran to her mother, who bent down and opened her arms to her! And then the little running child became my own crying form at the grill in Tours, and the English mother became my mother, as she turned and opened her arms to me!

Then Our Lady suddenly appeared in the painting, which now resembled the charcoal sketch I had drawn for our savages, her claw-hand clutching her cloak, her chin tucked behind her shoulder. It was I, not Gabriel, who knelt before her now, and she fixed on me, from behind that risen shoulder, a look of pure reproach, so that I cried in terror, "Lord, save me!"

With that the devil left me, as if I had exhaled him in my cry, and the pain returned to my body, recalling me to Jesus Christ and His adorable blood, and I picked up the paper again and though the cell was quite dark, the Lord made me able to write the Governor and in the light of day I could see that my hand was indeed legible, by His own miraculous will! No, I did not write my own words that night, but the Lord lit my way and sent my words, and the very next day warmed again the heart of the English jailer, who promised to deliver them.

Now my legs throbbed terribly, swelled, and finally began to bleed. Yes the blood was running there now, and I knew that He had answered my prayer. Yes, He told me, I have been listening to you all of this time; you have passed the test. I will soon send the glorious end that I have in mind for you.

To the High and Mighty Seigneur Phillippe de Rigaud,
Marquis de Vaudreuil, Chevalier de l'Ordre Militaire de
St. Louis and Governor General of New France.

Boston, 20 June 1706

Cher Seigneur,

WHILE CELEBRATING Mass in the city of Montréal last
month I was captured, and brought here to *Boston* as prisoner.
Yesterday I received word that you are negotiating with Governor Dudley for my release in exchange for the English girl
Marie-Ange (née Constance Baker).

I ask you, is the "kidnapping" of these English children
truly "diabolical" as the Governor would have it? For he is blind
to the glorious end we have in mind—the English see the children as theirs and theirs alone, when in truth they belong only to
God. Indeed, their precious souls, through no fault of their own,
would have no chance of being properly saved had they never
been captured.

It is true that their English parents suffer; they do not realize that they suffer even more for their misguided belief. Though
the children who pass through our missions may have fewer comforts, though their own families are divided, their end is good.
For they dwelt in sin and knew it not, having only those in thrall
to apostasy to guide them. Where they are, however, they are
no more infidels; they are baptized, and may one day give their
lives to the Lord in the convent; certainly those choosing to remain among the savages will at least be led in the ways of the true

church. *So we may ask, what is a mother on earth, in the face of a father for eternity?*

I beg you, Seigneur, in the name of Our Father, do not use me in this way; an exchange of my corporeal form for a tender one who has only just come to abjure the Calvinistic heresy could never be His will.

If it pleases God, may I die in this prison, for her soul's sake.

In in the Name of Him for Whom it is Most Glorious to Suffer
Father Simon René Floquart

From the Letter of Père de Launey

Boston, 12 July 1706

The tenth of July, 1706, I buried Father Simon René Floquart, aged sixty-three years.

P. de Launey, missionary

Skentsiese / Marie-Ange

IL EST OU, mon Pear?

Père de Jouy cried. He sat on the bench and held his face in his hands. *Ha' o ki wà hi,* said Aukwehtá:ku, holding out his arm.

She took his wrist and led him back along the path.

From the Relation of What Occurred in the Missions of the Society of Jesus in New France in the Year 1706; Letter of Father Jean de Jouy to the Reverend Father Superior of the Missions of the Society of Jesus in New France at Quebec

THE PEACE OF God!

His will has been fulfilled in withdrawing from the present trials of this life, our dear Père Simon René Floquart, who died last month in Boston, while a prisoner of the English.

According to Père de Launey who visited our Père Floquart in the jail more than once, this good man might take his place with our best martyrs of New France, for he refused to be traded by the English in exchange for the English girl whose soul he had secured for the Lord. Nonetheless, his letters are cheerful and describe none of what was later reported to us. Father de Launey relates that the jailer was at liberty to punish the prisoners at his own discretion for any offense, without a witness or permission from superiors. Thus, upon his staunch refusal to abjure his faith, Père Floquart was led with chains around his ankles to a stone confining cell too small for any man, but certainly for one of his bulk, and the only means to insert him was simply to shove his tender form, most brutally. The blood ran from his nose and eyes, his skin was abraded and raked by the stone, the chains around his ankles were so tightly bound that blood could not circulate to his feet, and a dropsy swelled his legs to such a degree that after being kept there for many days and nights (and still unwilling to abjure his faith) he could no longer walk.

Our Père Floquart bore great pain at the hands of this infidel jailer, who hated him for his love of Christ. We may be sure he bore it joyfully, for there is no higher suffering! And let us pray for this jailer, and any others who inflicted his wounds, as I am sure Father Floquart prayed, in the words of our Savior, *Pater, ignosce illis, non enim sciunt quod faciunt.*

Your Very Humble and Obedient Servant in Our Lord!
Jean de Jouy, Priest

Final Entry, the Commonplace Book
of John Baker

I HAVE come to the end of my commonplace book.

As I have written here, with God's help I devised a plan for my daughter's redemption. The Governor Dudley was most helpful in ordering the abduction of the priest who lived in her mission, and after the deed was done, the French governor most willing for the jailed priest to be exchanged for my daughter. All had passed wonderfully.

Then came word that the priest had refused the exchange.

Truly the Lord had withdrawn His face from me. I prayed all day and into the night, examining my soul as well as my little library, seeking a sign. So it happened that I came across this passage below, most troubling, which I had passed over, choosing instead to copy here *many* things of a contrary sense, as they pertain to Children

Per JOHN LOCKE, *Some Thoughts Concerning Education*

I am very apt to think, that great severity of punishment does but very little good, nay, great harm in education; and I believe it will be found that, *caeteris paribus*, those children who have been most chastis'd, seldom make the best men. . . .

For I advise their parents and governors always to carry this in their minds, that children are to be treated as rational creatures. . . . We must look upon them to be like ourselves, with the same passions, the same desires. We would be thought rational creatures, and have our freedom; we love not to be uneasy under constant rebukes and brow-beatings, nor can we bear severe humours and great distance in those we converse with. Whoever has such treatment when he is a man, will look out other company, other friends, other conversation, with whom he can be at ease.

I was overcome with chagrin. Had I erred in my attempts to ensure my daughter's salvation? After reading Mr. Locke I could not sleep for my despair, and thumbed through many other books, finding no consolation, only warnings of keeping such a book as I had, of "over much knowledge," in the words of Seigneur de Montaigne, as "the Stoics forbid also that which comes from the exercise of the minde, and require a bridle to it!"

At this I stopped my reading, and lay my head upon my desk and slept fitfully there that night.

In the morning the door creaked open and a soft beam of light fell into my study. I sat up. Through the door walked the little orange cat. He jumped onto the chair next to my desk, which was also now bathed in that beam of light, and curled himself around a book with a worn red cover that had sat upon that chair for many months, The *Confessiones* of Augustine of Hippo, there bowing his little forehead upon the spine and falling instantly to sleep. I gently slid the book from under the cat (he stirred, then resumed his purring), and I perceived that I had read this book before. How else had it found its place on the chair, if I had not placed it there? And if I had in fact placed it there, would I not have opened it? At the same time, as I began to read, I could not be sure. Perhaps the words were new to me!

In fact, to God there is not much difference in our learning or remembering, and when our forgetting occurs, it is also His pleasure, for if words are dear to Him (which I knew somehow that morning, these were), He will keep them, on our behalf, for all time.

Though as I write this, I think instead it is the essence of the words that He keeps on our behalf, which is not manifest, and comes before a sort of schism that occurs when we write or think in some particular tongue.

No matter.

Enough!

What follows is that dear account, with which I close my book, and the story of my daughter's redemption withal:

As a young man, Augustine of Hippo was deep in heresy, under the sway of the Manicheans. His devout mother went crying to a certain bishop, and begged him to win her son's soul for the Lord. But this holy man refused, assuring the mother, that her son needed no priest to convince him, but would come to know by the light of truth, which already resided in him, the right way to go.

Still the mother cried, overcome by her anguish regarding her son's soul, until the priest lost patience with this good woman.

Go your way, said he. It is impossible that that the child of these tears should perish.

Skentsiese / Marie-Ange

IN A DREAM she was walking through the wilderness again. She was alone, and the fog was thick, and she could not see the path in front of her. She only knew that she must find her way home.

Then the fog lifted. She stood on the bank of a river. It was not the one they had marched along, for there were trees on the opposite bank, and their long boughs bent into the water. Before them stood the Pear. Oh, yes. He had died in the other world, but here he was alive, and speaking to her, telling her how to go home. Yet his words were in a strange tongue, and she could not understand them. On he spoke, so that there was more and more she could not understand. And she was dismayed, for she had walked and walked and was so very tired, and must go home and did not know the way. So she began to cry.

Seeing this, he smiled at her. His face was glowing, for in his cupped palms he held a ball of light. It shone on his skin and through his fingers and out into the water as he stretched out his arms, so that she might take it from him.

Then she woke. She sat up on her bench and remembered. She was already home.

Letter from Deacon Sheldon
to Governor Dudley

3 January 1707/8

Sir,

I AM GLAD to report that all six of the English children newly
captivated last year have been redeemed, by the Grace of God
(Alexander, Brown, Stilson, Rising, Harris, Wells.) As for the
daughter of John Baker, I have delivered the letters from the
girl's mother to the fort near Montreal, and did read all to her,
as I have promised.

The girl's mother had been certain that the sight of the letters themselves, written in her hand, should move her daughter
to return with me. Alas, the girl did not look long upon them, and
when I had done, spoke only to the priest, who relayed again that
she would not come, as she has said formerly. Her appearance is
still savage, as her father had described it, although in truth she is
more so a young savage woman now, rather than a child.

May God keep her poor parents.

Your Humble Servant,
Deacon John Sheldon

*God's great Providence and enduring mercies as occasioned
by the terable captivitie and wonderfull redemption of
Sarah Baker (John Baker his wife) of Hartfield Falls,
the Colony of Massachusetts Bay in the English America,
having been captivated by most barbarous salvages and
carried, with her daughter, to Canada*

Epilogue

IT IS WITH heavy heart, dear reader, that I offer this, the account of my trials, as a caution for the reader.

Perhaps we two are merely God's *ornaments*; for my Constance the seed was sown but Satan taketh away; and for me though the plant full grown, yet the vanities and cares of the world did choke it, for as I waited to finish this account, so that it might have a different end, I did not accept what I must, that *if any man come to me and hate not his father, and mother, and wife, and children, and brethren, and sisters, yea, and his own life also, he cannot be my disciple.*

If her Reprobation is certain with Him, no plea will convince her to return. It was divine providence that made Noah worthy of his task; by that same providence Shem invoked demons, and taught others to do the same, though surely it wrung his father's heart; so we must only trust that *nothing happens but what God has knowingly and willingly decreed.*

~

THEN SHE WAS in the English house again. Its shelves went high into the dark trees, above the mist, and into the mountains. It was so vast that all those who entered might find there what they had lost. And there was room too, for all that had passed upon the earth, every moment and minute of every day.

Through the planks of the floor she heard them singing.

Hannah, John, Ezariah. Mother, Father, Pear. They sang as one, for where they were there was no cleaving. Oh, the song was most delightful. So following it she walked to the cellar and was not afraid.

She opened the door, and the light flooded up.

Acknowledgments

I am deeply grateful to many people who made this book possible by lending their expertise and support: David Sgarlata, Martha Bohrer, Randy Casperson, Beth McGowan, Katie and Mike Shea, Chris Mann, Connie Kuntz, Blue Montakhab, Joe O'Malley, and my husband Dan Libman, who also happens to be my favorite writer. Many thanks also to Gregory Wolfe for his meticulous care in steering this book in the right direction and giving it such a fitting home.

This fictional story is inspired by the life of Eunice Williams (Marguerite Kanenstenhawi Arosen), a young English colonist taken captive in a raid on Deerfield, Massachusetts in 1704. I could not have written it without the guidance of *The Unredeemed Captive*, by John Demos. I recommend this remarkable book to anyone who would like to know more about Eunice's real story and its historical context.

This book was set in IM Fell, digitized by Igino Marini, based on the typeface used by Bishop of Oxford John Fell in the late seventeenth century for Oxford University Press, and in Warnock Pro, designed by Robert Slimbach.

This book was designed by Shannon Carter, Ian Creeger, and Gregory Wolfe. It was published in hardcover, paperback, and electronic formats by Slant Books, Seattle, Washington.

Cover images generated by ChatGPT based on eighteenth-century woodcuts.

www.ingramcontent.com/pod-product-compliance
Lightning Source LLC
Chambersburg PA
CBHW031102020726
47495CB00007B/2009